Other Books by Susan Kelly

THE GEMINI MAN

THE SUMMERTIME SOLDIERS

TRAIL OF THE DRAGON

UNTIL PROVEN INNOCENT

AND SOON I'LL COME TO KILL YOU

AND SOON I'LL COME TO KILL YOU

SUSAN KELLY

VILLARD BOOKS   NEW YORK   1991

Library of Congress Cataloging-in-Publication Data

Kelly, Susan.
     And soon I'll come to kill you / Susan Kelly. — 1st ed.
          p.   cm.
     ISBN 0-394-58415-5
     I. Title.
   PS3561.E39715A82   1991
   813'.54—dc20   90-28833
9 8 7 6 5 4 3 2
First edition

AND SOON
I'LL COME
TO KILL YOU

1

The first letter arrived on October sixteenth. I read it and dismissed it.

My name is Elizabeth Connors. I'm a free-lance writer. Writers get mail from their readers. Most of it is charming—people telling you they liked your last book or the article you published in the August issue of *Boston Magazine*. Sometimes they want to point out an error they think you've made. Or, since I write fiction as well as nonfiction, suggest a story idea.

Every once in a while, you'll get a critical letter.

And occasionally you'll get one that's really weird. Like borderline psychotic weird. I remember a handwritten note from some guy in Portland, Maine. Two pages of literate, flattering commentary on an article I'd published in *New England Monthly*. How nice, I thought. The last line of the letter read, "Send me a picture of yourself, naked except for black patent-leather high-heeled boots."

Maybe if I wrote about fashion or home decor, I wouldn't attract that kind of attention. I'm positive I wouldn't if I'd stayed in my former profession, teaching college English.

What I write about is crime. And in the six years I've been doing that, I've received a dozen or so letters reviling me for being: a) sick, b) disgusting, or c) evil. These were all in response to newspaper or magazine features I'd written on truly horrendous cases like ritual murder or child rapes. Maybe my correspondents thought I committed those atrocities as well. Or condoned them. Who knows? I was always tempted to write back to each and every one of the irate twits and say that I didn't *make* the news, I just reported it. But I never did. And none of them ever wrote to me again, as far as I could tell.

All that should explain why, on the nice sunny October morning I slit open the white three-by-five envelope and took out a single sheet of paper that had printed on it, "You vicious bitch," I wasn't terribly shocked. A bit taken aback, yes. But not shocked or horrified.

The letter had been delivered along with a VISA bill, an invitation to a gallery opening, and some supermarket circulars.

I looked again at the envelope. No return address. A Boston postmark. My name and address were block-printed in pencil. The letter bore neither signature nor salutation. No date. I looked at the envelope. It had been postmarked the day before.

The printing on both envelope and letter was small and neat and very dark. Whoever had held the pencil had wielded considerable pressure. Not enough to tear the paper, but almost.

Another born-again cuckoo clock, I figured. Probably somebody angry about that article I'd done recently on child pornography. Or that one on the doctor who'd sexually assaulted his elderly female patients. I tossed the letter onto the pile of normal mail on the kitchen table.

I was afterward to wonder why I hadn't just pitched it into the trash.

The next letter came two days later. Same envelope and paper. Identical pencil printing. And the same three-word message: "You vicious bitch."

Two in a row, obviously from the same source, made me a little queasy. Not alarmed. But I figured there wouldn't be any harm in showing both letters to Jack.

"They're probably not from the Portland Pervert," was his first response.

"Not the same style," I agreed. "Still . . . you think this is something for me to worry about?"

Jack frowned slightly. Then he shook his head. "No. Not if it stops with this. Or doesn't escalate to threats." He nodded at the two letters on his desk blotter. "Clowns like this are like obscene callers. That's how they get their rocks off. They never *do* anything. Not usually, anyway."

I smiled. "What I figured."

"All the same," Jack continued, "leave these with me."

"Of course," I said. "If I get murdered by some loonie, they might be a good lead."

Jack just looked at me. I laughed.

Letter Number Three arrived on Saturday. It read:

> I bet you think I'm just some anonymous freak, don't you, bitch? Well, I'm not.
>
> Are you getting nervous? You should be.

I let out my breath in a long, soft *whooo* and slipped the letter back into the envelope.

Jack was coming to my place for dinner. I handed him the letter along with his drink. I watched him as he read it. His face seemed to harden.

"Well?" I said.

He put the letter on the coffee table. "This is my business now," he said.

What he meant by "his business" was law-enforcement business. Jack is John Lingemann, a detective-lieutenant in the Cambridge Police Department. I've known him for six years. We're not married and we don't live together. We're a lot closer than many couples who do—maybe precisely because we're also separate. I don't analyze the situation. I just enjoy it.

Letter Number Four came in Monday's mail. It was longer than the previous three. And creepier.

> You must be wondering what all this is about, bitch. Well, sooner or later, you'll find out. And when you do, you'll be sorry. Sorrysorrysorrysorry.

> In fact, you'll be dead. Think about that, bitch. Think about it *hard*.

I stared at the paper until the individual letters on it lost their meaning and became just little random markings on a white field.

Sorrysorrysorrysorry.

I hand-carried the letter in a shopping bag to the police station, up to Jack's office in the Criminal Investigation Division on the third floor. He was shuffling through a pile of arrest/incident reports when I appeared in his doorway. I dangled the shopping bag by its handle before me and said, "My unknown admirer's just had another attack of epistolary fever."

Jack held out a hand across the desk. "Let me see."

I gave him the bag.

He read the letter once very quickly and then a second time very slowly, as if examining and memorizing each word. Then he opened a desk drawer and got out a large manila envelope with a plastic window in it. The envelope had the word EVIDENCE printed across the front. He dropped the letter into the envelope. "Right," he said. "Here's what you do. Go home, pack a bag, switch on your answering machine, round up the dog, and go to my place."

I was so startled by the uncharacteristic peremptoriness of his tone—and the bluntness of the order—that all I said was, "Huh?"

"You heard me."

"Yeah. I did. Go to your place. And—what? Stay there?"

"Uh-huh."

"And not come out for the next three years?"

He looked irritated. "Just think of it as a temporary security measure."

I stared at him in disbelief. "But I have work to do."

"So you can do it in my apartment. There's plenty of room."

I didn't say anything.

"Liz," Jack added, "this joker knows where you live. And obviously he's not too tightly wrapped."

I laughed in the way you do when you're totally aghast. "Jack, just the other day you told me these letters probably weren't anything to worry about."

"Your life wasn't being threatened, then."

"Oh, really. What can this clown do? Send me a letter bomb?"

"Try, break into your bedroom some night, rape you, and slit your throat."

"But my dog's always on the alert. She—"

"Has a great bark and no bite."

I sighed. "Look, Jack, I *am* taking these letters seriously. But I think you're taking them *too* seriously."

He shook his head. Then he tapped his forefinger on the evidence envelope. "This is something I've had more experience with than you."

"Well, of course. And therefore you know that ninety percent of threats like those turn out to be hot air. Don't they?"

"Sure. It's the other ten percent that concerns me." He tapped the evidence envelope again. "This sounds like the other ten percent."

"How can you tell?"

He shrugged. Then he rose and went to the office door. He thrust head and shoulders into the main C.I.D. office and said, "Sam? Can you come in here?"

He returned to the desk. "Let's get a second opinion, okay?"
"Sure."

A moment later a sergeant named Flaherty came into the office. He was a tall skinny guy in his mid-fifties with russet hair fading to gray and a long jowly face permanently graven with Celtic melancholy. Except when he smiled, as he did now at me. He was Jack's closest friend in the police department and probably, with the exception of me, in the world.

"Yo, baby," I said, and hopped up to give him a hug. He kissed me on the cheek. Jack watched this little byplay with something less than patience.

Flaherty sat down in the other spare chair, crossed his legs, and fumbled in his jacket pocket. He took out a pack of cigarettes and, in defiance of Cambridge's no smoking in public buildings ordinance, lit one.

Jack handed Flaherty the evidence envelope. "Take a look at this. Liz got it in this morning's mail."

I noticed that Flaherty read the letter the exact same way Jack had—a quick run-through followed by a slow study. When he'd finished, he tucked it carefully back into the evidence envelope. Also like Jack, he held the paper only by its very edges.

Flaherty tossed the manila envelope onto the desk.

"Jack seems to think I'm in serious danger," I said.

Flaherty was silent for a moment. Then he said, "I'm with Jack on that, kid."

I glanced at Jack. He was watching me steadily, his face expressionless.

"I seen the crackpot stuff before," Flaherty said. "And I seen the real stuff." He nodded at the evidence envelope. "That don't look like a joke to me."

I took a deep breath.

"I also read the other three letters you got," Flaherty continued. "Jack showed me." He doused his cigarette in the battered green metal ashtray that sat on the corner of the desk. "I was you, I'd take some precautions."

I jerked a thumb at Jack. "Like move in with him?"

Flaherty raised his eyebrows. "Wouldn't be a bad idea."

"Swell," I said flatly.

Flaherty stood up and stretched. "Gotta run," he said. He gave me a pat on the shoulder and ambled out of the office.

I made a sour face at Jack. "What'd you do, coach him before I came in?"

Jack laughed. "I can parade four more cops in here, two of them women, who'll tell you exactly the same thing Sam did."

"Sure." I pulled my jacket off the back of my chair and wriggled into it. "I'll be running along, too."

My tone was a little cold and my movements a little abrupt. Jack seemed taken aback.

"I have errands," I said. I didn't elaborate.

He nodded. Then he said, "Be careful."

I closed my eyes and exhaled loudly, feeling myself teetering on the ragged edge of exasperation. "Yeah, you better lend me your gun so I can blow away the fifty homicidal maniacs ready to jump me soon's I leave this building."

"One would be enough."

"Right." I rose. "See you later."

"Uh-huh."

When I was at the door, Jack said, "Liz?"

I turned. "Yes?"

He had his hands linked behind his head and was leaning back in his chair. "Remember Stephen Larrain?"

I stiffened. "Of course."

"Remember what happened to him?"

"Yes."

Jack said nothing further. There was no need.

I pushed through the swinging door of the C.I.D. and went down the cast-iron stairs. I walked slowly, my head bent.

Stephen Larrain.

Like me, Larrain had been a writer. Like me, he had written about crime.

Fourteen years ago, Larrain had published a scathing series of articles on the illegal doings of a local real estate developer. In return, the developer had had Larrain murdered. Larrain had been sitting at the kitchen table in his Cambridge apartment, working on a story, when the hired killer had burst through the back door, pointed a shotgun at him, and splattered Larrain all over the cabinets and refrigerator.

I worked in my kitchen, too. And I had a back door.

Be nice if the resemblance between Larrain and me stayed limited to that.

David Epstein is a forensic psychiatrist. Three mornings a week, he works out of the clinic at the Middlesex County courthouse. One of his jobs is to evaluate people accused of doing things like chopping their entire families to bits with axes, to see if they're competent to stand trial. He knows a crazy when he meets one. He is also familiar with the little tricks the noncrazy pull in order to appear demented.

When I left Jack's office, I called Epstein and invited him to lunch.

In my handbag, I had photocopies of all four letters and the envelopes in which they'd arrived. The copies were excellent, a product of the machine in the police department's Records and Identification Bureau.

I met Epstein at the trendy delicatessen in the basement of the restored American Twine Company building on Third Street.

He'd gotten there ahead of me and grabbed a nice table for two in a corner. He rose as I came toward him and bent down to kiss my cheek. He was about six-two, and heavyset. Black hair and beard, sharp dark brown eyes and swarthy skin. A Levantine brigand disguised as a shrink.

We sat. There was food on the table, several pint and half-pint containers of different kinds of pasta and vegetable salads, plus plastic forks and Styrofoam plates.

"I ordered all my favorites," Epstein said. "Hope you don't mind."

"Not at all," I said. "Looks good. But I'm paying."

"Liz, I spent this morning talking to a nineteen-year-old imbecile who raped his seven-year-old sister and then doused her with kerosene and tried to set fire to her."

"Jesus!"

"So," Epstein continued, "when I say lunch is my treat, I mean that in more ways than one."

"This, uh, imbecile. Is he—he must be very sick."

Epstein put some rotini-olive-pepperoni-cheese mixture on his plate. He looked up at me. "Not the way you probably mean. I was using the word *imbecile* loosely. He's competent to be tried, and to participate in his own defense. Legally he's sane. Morally he's out somewhere in a realm you and I couldn't even begin to imagine."

I helped myself to some cold rice with carrots, peas, green olives, black olives, tomatoes, and green peppers and to the spinach-and-mushroom salad. "I thought psychiatrists didn't deal with moral issues."

"Call it what you like," Epstein said. "This kid needs to be put away for a long, long time. Or maybe just fed slowly into a giant meat grinder, feet first. When he went after his sister, he was out on bail for raping another girl."

"Another *child*?"

"Fifteen years old," Epstein replied. "Seems like childhood to me, babe."

"God," I muttered.

"Cheer up," Epstein said. "There's a bright side. This crud will get convicted, and he'll probably die in prison."

I raised my eyebrows.

"The other inmates will kill him."

I nodded. "Of course. Child-rapists give other criminals a bad name."

"Uh-huh."

We ate without further conversation for a few minutes. I finished what was on my plate and took some of the rotini salad. The restaurant was starting to fill up, mostly with people from the local high-tech firms and the courthouse. I saw an assistant district attorney I knew and waved to her.

"David?"

"Yes?"

I nudged my empty plate aside. "I've been getting some very strange mail lately."

"Oh?"

I reached into my purse for the photocopies and handed them to Epstein. He fumbled in his inside suitcoat pocket for a pair of half-glasses, put them on, and began to read. Then he looked up at me. "Somebody out there doesn't like you."

"Yeah, I gathered," I said dryly.

He put the letters down on the table. "You want me to tell you whether whoever wrote those things is crazy? I can't do that."

I nodded.

"What do you think?"

I was startled. "Me? Oh—well, God, David, I don't know. I mean . . ." I reached over, picked up the letters, and fanned through them. "The person who wrote them is literate, anyway. There're no grammar or spelling or punctuation errors. The last two letters even have a sort of distinctive style to them. Like, rhythmic."

"I noticed that, too."

I smiled. "Well, then, maybe my enemy is another writer."

"Could be. You know of anyone really jealous of you?"

"Oh, David. I was joking. Who do you think I am? Judith Krantz? Jackie Collins? Stephen King? I'm not exactly rich and famous. Have you seen me on Carson or Oprah or Donahue lately? If I ever did get on TV, it'd be on Letterman between Stupid Pet Tricks and Monkey Cam."

"Success is relative. So is fame." Epstein poked in the rotini salad container and fished out a quarter-sized slice of pepperoni. "I read things written by you all the time. I see your picture in the papers and in magazines. Take some person who's been writing for fifteen years and yet never managed to get anything published. To that person, you might be really big time."

I laughed, a little uncomfortably. "And that would make him jealous enough to start writing me threats?"

Epstein tilted his head. "What makes you think it's a *him* and not a *her?*"

2

I spent that afternoon shoving all the files and notebooks and clippings relating to the various articles I was currently working on into a cardboard box and slinging clothing and toiletries into a suitcase. Lucy, my runt chocolate Lab/Weimaraner cross, watched with great interest and mounting excitement. She always associated the act of me packing with the prospect of the two of us going for a car ride somewhere (anywhere), an event she likes as well as she does eating, sleeping, and chasing squirrels.

"I'm glad *you're* happy about this," I said to her. She raised her tail and waved it. I threw some jeans and a sweater into the suitcase.

David Epstein had also thought it an extremely good idea that I move in with Jack for a while.

The hell of it was, he, Flaherty, and Jack were probably right. I'd grudgingly conceded that much over the course of the day. Their combined professional knowledge of people who made violent threats—and carried them out—was a lot greater than mine. And they all seemed convinced I was in danger.

For the best of practical reasons I had to abandon my own turf.

Shit.

When I'd finished packing, I wandered around the apartment. It was only three rooms—given Cambridge rents, I couldn't afford anything more—but they were *nice* rooms, large and high-ceilinged. The living room had a bay window and a fireplace. And built-in bookcases. Off the kitchen was a deck with a staircase that led down to an enclosed backyard in which Lucy could boogie around to her heart's content.

Anyway, this place wasn't just where I lived. It was where I worked, and had for eight years.

The thought of being driven out of it enraged me.

The irony was that, under other circumstances, I would have looked forward to moving in for a little while with Jack. We stayed together on the weekends, taking turns at each other's houses, and had great times. But we did that because we wanted to, not because we had to.

Damn.

I dragged my luggage into the living room and deposited it on the floor beside the cardboard box of writing materials. Lucy lay down next to the suitcase (presumably so I wouldn't forget her when I left) and grinned at me.

"I'm glad you're happy," I repeated.

She thumped her tail once on the rug and then rested her muzzle on her forepaws. Her eyelids drooped. I've always envied the capacity dogs have to go virtually instantaneously from a state of high excitement to one of total torpidity.

If Lucy could relax, I probably should, too. No point in fidgeting around the house. I flopped down on the couch.

I subscribe to a lot of magazines, and the most recent ones were stacked on the coffee table before me. I hadn't gotten around to reading any of them yet, and I had an hour and a half to burn. Might as well catch up on things. I hefted the top half of the pile into my lap.

I flipped through *Time, Newsweek, Vanity Fair, The New Republic, GQ, Spy, Esquire, Boston Magazine, New York, Chicago, New West,* and *Texas Monthly.* A number of articles looked interesting. I started to read several, but found I couldn't concentrate on any of them.

I picked up the remaining magazines on the coffee table. At the top of that pile was a quarterly devoted to the concerns and interests of the woman journalist. I opened it and glanced at the table of contents. Again, the titles of a few articles caught my eye. And again, I couldn't settle down and get through one.

I closed the magazine. The cover photo was of a woman with short dark hair, a narrow triangular face, and a wide, happy smile. The cutline beneath the photo read: "The Short Life and Long Death of Anita Kittredge."

I pulled the magazine back into my lap and stared at the photo.

I had never known Anita Kittredge, but I knew who she was. So did every other woman crime writer in the country. Her story was imprinted on our brains.

Anita Kittredge was thirty-three years old. She had started as a reporter at a Minneapolis newspaper a month after her graduation from the University of Minnesota. Her first assignment had been to the Arts and Leisure pages, for which she'd covered the theater, movies, galleries, and concerts. From there she'd moved to the Metro section of the paper, doing general reporting. The first big crime story she'd covered had been the trial of a man accused of murdering his estranged wife and their three children. So thorough and detailed had been her account that the city editor had assigned her permanently to the court and police beat. And there her star had really begun to rise. The following year she did an investigative series on corruption in the judiciary that earned her an award from the Midwest Press Association. Some people predicted she would win a Pulitzer before the age of thirty.

That never happened. Anita Kittredge spent the evening of her twenty-ninth birthday interviewing a physics professor, the victim of an apparent serial rapist who selected as his victims only fairly high-powered professional women. The interviewee had been the sixth such person to be attacked.

Anita was the seventh.

The rapist got two more women before the police got him. The prosecution contended at his trial that the defendant had chosen bright, educated, successful women as his prey because he had a profound hatred of feminists. He had in fact made statements before witnesses that all "these women" deserved punishment for their "crimes" against men.

The defendant was a graduate student in clinical psychology at the University of Minnesota. He felt that a fellowship he should rightfully have been given had gone to a woman simply because she was female rather than the more qualified recipient.

He pled not guilty by reason of insanity. He was convicted of six of the rapes, including Anita's, largely on the basis of forensic evidence, and sentenced to twenty-five years in the state prison.

Anita didn't attend the trial. She was in a rehabilitation hospital. So severely had the rapist beaten her before and after the actual sexual assault that he had stove in the entire left side of her head.

The damage was permanent. Three years after she was supposed to have won the Pulitzer, Anita Kittredge was in a wheelchair. She could slightly move one arm and one leg. She had to be fed and dressed and washed. Intellectually she functioned on the level of a first-grader.

I sat very quietly while this memory tape unspooled in my mind.

Of course Anita Kittredge hadn't been destroyed *precisely* because she'd been a crime writer. She'd been destroyed for being smart and ambitious and good at her job.

So what? The distinction made no difference.

It didn't make me feel less edgy to recall that Anita Kittredge, like Stephen Larrain, had been attacked in her own apartment.

I got up from the sofa and moved to the bay window, where I stood gazing unseeingly down at the street. My resistance to the idea of moving in with Jack had very little to do with sense of self. I'd been fending for myself my entire adult life. The only man ever to contribute to my support had been my father. I didn't have to prove to anyone—least of all myself—that I was tough. I didn't need to take stupid risks just to show the world that I was a grown-up independent girl.

When you're as tall as I am (five foot ten), people assume that anyway. And act accordingly. It's impossible for me to identify with women who complain that men constantly want to protect them. That urge wasn't one I normally aroused in the male breast.

What I resented (ferociously) about *this* situation was the sudden limitation that had been placed on my personal freedom.

At four-thirty I fed the dog. Then I read the article on Anita Kittredge until Jack came to pick up Lucy and me a little after five.

We ordered food in from a Chinese restaurant. Afterward we had coffee in the living room. Jack had a fireplace, too. We used it. The night was chilly.

Jack lay on the floor watching the flames. I watched him. At forty-five, he was eight years older than I. Except for the dusting of gray in his thick brown hair, he looked younger than he actually was. He was built long and lean and well-muscled. The firelight threw the strong bones of his face into high prominence.

He must have felt my gaze, because he turned his head in my direction and smiled.

"So," he said. "How do you like living together, so far?"

I glanced at my watch. "It's only been three hours."

He laughed. "Didn't we once spend an entire week together without driving each other insane?"

"That was for different reasons."

"Yeah. Still, it's a good omen."

I cleared my throat. "Jack?"

"Hmmm?" He was back to watching the fire.

"I'm not going to stay shut up in this apartment twenty-four hours a day. I have a life to lead. I'm going to keep on doing that."

He was silent a moment. Then he said, "Well, okay. Sure. I expected you would."

"I'll keep an eye out when I leave the house. But I *do* plan to keep going out."

He nodded.

"Whoever this moron is who's sending me the letters, I can't let him dictate my existence."

"No." He pushed himself into a sitting position, then rose and went to the couch. I followed him with my eyes.

"You're not happy about that, are you?" I asked.

He leaned back on the couch and put his feet on the coffee table. "With you running around loose and some nut after you? No, I can't say the thought thrills me."

I sighed, caught between exasperation and appreciation for his concern. "I don't think anybody will shoot me or stab me in the post office or the library."

He smiled reluctantly. "Probably not. But why take unnecessary chances?"

"That's my point, Jack. I'm not going to."

He nodded. "Sure."

We drank our coffee. Lucy paced into the room and lay down on the rug before the fireplace. She chose the spot Jack had just vacated.

"I wonder, was she waiting in the hall for me to move my carcass?" he asked.

I laughed, more out of relief at the break in the tension between us than in amusement at the dog's antics. "No doubt. Listen, Jack. I had lunch with David Epstein today. You want to hear what we talked about?"

"All right."

I recited the conversation.

When I'd finished, Jack put his head back and stared at the ceiling. "Ah, I suppose it could be an unsuccessful writer," he mused. "Cambridge and Boston are full of them, right? Don't know, though. It just seems to me more likely that whoever sent you those four letters is somebody you wrote about."

"Uh-huh. A criminal whose case I followed in one of my articles. And now he—or she—is out of the slammer and wants revenge."

"It's happened to other writers and reporters. Why not to you?"

"Yes." I set my coffee cup on the end table. Then I picked up the briefcase I'd put on the floor beside my chair. I heaved it into my lap and opened it. "That's why I made up this list of all the true-crime pieces I've written and had published in the past six years. Plus where and when they appeared, with a paragraph summary of each article and the names of all the principals. Ta-da."

"I've said it before and I'll say it again," Jack remarked. "You think like a cop. Now gimme that list."

In keeping with my policy of leading a normal life, Tuesday at five I met one of my closest women friends, Christine Cameron, for a drink in the Parker House bar. The genteel upstairs bar, not the noisy downstairs one where all the politicians gathered.

Christine is a communications expert in the Boston office of an international consulting firm. Like me, she used to teach college English. Like me, she writes. The difference is, she writes about business, and does so less frequently than I. But then, she has a marriage and a ten-hour-a-day job to distract her.

I'd made this date with Chris well before I'd started getting the letters. We had stuff to catch up on. I let her go first. When she asked me what was new in *my* life, I told her.

She blinked. Then she said, "Jesus."

I fished the letters from my purse and scaled them across the cocktail table at her. "You're the communications maven. Tell me what *you* think."

She read the letters, frowning. Then she folded the papers and let them drop into her lap.

"Boy," she said. "These are almost as bad as some of the student evaluations I used to get."

"Yeah." I laughed. "I thought the same thing, too. But it's been a long time since I taught. And while some of my kids were a little slow on the uptake, it probably wouldn't take them this long to decide to avenge themselves for the D or the F they got in freshman comp."

"Unlikely," Christine agreed. She glanced again at the letters. "Anyway, vile as these are, they don't look as if they were written by a dummy."

"That was my reaction."

Christine sucked in her upper lip. "Liz, can I ask you a blunt question?"

"It wouldn't be the first time."

She smiled briefly. Then she cocked her head. "Have you made a play for or a pass at anyone's husband or boyfriend recently?"

I nearly spilled my drink. "*What?*"

Christine held up her hand like a traffic cop. "All right, all right. Don't get excited. I didn't mean it that way."

I scowled. "Well, what way did you mean it?"

"All I'm saying is, is there any time recently that you were at, oh, I don't know, like a party, say, and you got into a long conversation with a man, and he was really enjoying talking to you, and maybe the woman he was with noticed what a good time he was having with you and . . ." Christine let her voice trail off meaningfully.

"Yes," I said irritably. "Yes, I have been to parties recently. And yes, I have at those parties engaged in conversation with various male guests. And yes, they appeared to be at least not totally bored talking to me. And no, I did not try to slap a make on any one of them."

"I didn't say you did," Christine replied patiently. "Not deliberately or consciously. I know how you feel about Jack. But that's beside the point. Maybe the wife of one of the guys you talked to thought you were trying to slap a make on her husband." Christine shrugged, very lightly but very expressively. "And that he'd take you up on it."

"So the wife would start writing me threatening letters as a result?"

Christine sighed. "Liz, it could be a woman whose husband hasn't said two words to her in seven years. Or who cheats on her constantly. If you were in that position, wouldn't it make you crazy enough to start doing something drastic, finally?"

"No, because I'd dump any bastard like that in two seconds."

"Sure you would," Christine said. "And I would, too. But the kind of woman I'm talking about couldn't. And unfortunately there are still a fairly large number of such women around."

I shook my head. "Why? Why does that kind of woman stay with that kind of man?"

"Oh, Liz, your guess is as good as mine. Because those

women don't know anything else to do. Or how to do anything else. They were raised not to function alone, so they can't. Another thing . . ."

I looked at her. "What?"

Christine raised her glass to her mouth, but didn't drink from it. "They learned that the best way to be attractive to men was to be passive and dependent. And the lesson paid off for them, at least initially."

"And afterward?"

"What they didn't learn was that men get tired of passive and dependent and start looking for the opposite after a while."

"So?"

Christine sipped her drink. "You're the opposite."

"But I haven't *done* anything."

"It's nothing you do," she said. "It's what you are."

I folded my hands together. "In that case," I said, "why should the woman blame me?"

Christine's answering smile was even briefer than her previous one. And a little sad.

I ordered another round.

On the subway back to Jack's, I tried to sort it all out.

A failed writer, David Epstein had suggested.

A vengeful criminal, Jack had proposed.

A wronged wife, Christine had theorized.

The train noise was a rumbling monotonous counterpoint to my thoughts.

Sorrysorrysorrysorry.

The fifth letter arrived on Wednesday. The only real surprise was that it was delivered to Jack's house. It was addressed to me in care of him, Lieutenant John Lingemann. And it said:

Did you think that was a smart move, bitch, hiding out at your boyfriend's? Don't you know that I know where you are at all times? Because I do. There's nowhere you can go that I won't find you.

And soon I'll come to kill you.

I had spent that morning working in Jack's study, so I was there when the mail came at noon. I knew what the letter was before I opened it. Those cheap white three-by-five envelopes and the small neat dark pencil printing had become very familiar.

Jack came home for lunch. I handed him the envelope as he walked in the door.

We didn't eat. Instead, we sat in the kitchen, the letter on the table before us, taking the place of sandwiches and coffee.

"God," I said. "Do you suppose whoever this is"—I gestured at the letter—"followed me over here from my place? Or followed us the night you picked me up?"

"Either that," Jack said, "or he made a damn good guess that if you weren't living in your apartment any longer, you'd be staying with me."

"But that means he, whoever, knows you, too," I said. "And what our relationship is."

"That's right."

I looked at the kitchen windows. They were locked. The door leading out to the back porch was deadbolted. All were connected to a burglar alarm, as were the front door and living room, bedroom, study, and bathroom windows. And the door to the basement.

That fact seemed slightly less reassuring than it had before the noon mail delivery.

What was going through my mind seemed to be going through Jack's, for he said, "Maybe it's not too hot an idea for you to spend too much time alone here during the day."

I nodded. Then I glanced at the dog, curled up on the floor in front of the stove. "What about her? Can *she* stay here by herself? I really would die if somebody broke in here and— hurt her."

Jack shook his head. "Don't worry. I can fix it up with my landlord to look after her when you and I aren't around. It'll be okay. She likes him and he likes her."

"All right."

Jack pushed back his chair and rose. "In the meantime, come back to the station with me. I have something I want you to do."

"What's that?"

He took a deep breath and shoved the chair back into place beneath the table. "Learn how to use a gun."

The lesson lasted an hour. I already knew the basics. I had, in fact, had previous opportunity to fire a gun. What I was doing now was qualifying to shoot to kill legally. There would be no difficulty involved in my obtaining a permit to carry a gun. I wasn't insane and I wasn't a convicted felon.

Afterward Jack had to go out on the street. I had a cup of coffee in the C.I.D. with Sam Flaherty and a young patrol officer named Larry Gotovich.

The news that my life had been threatened had spread pretty much throughout the department. If there were an Olympic Freestyle Gossiping Team, it would be made up entirely of cops.

Flaherty had already seen Letter Number Five. He described the contents to Gotovich. Gotovich made a face. Then he said, "Nice."

"Yeah."

Gotovich turned to me. "You got any idea who it might be?"

I shrugged.

He regarded his coffee cup thoughtfully. "You do something to piss off one of your neighbors? Like play loud music late at night? Like that? Your dog been shitting in somebody else's yard?"

I burst out laughing. Flaherty stared at Gotovich as though he suspected the kid might be brain-damaged.

"No," I said. "I can plead innocent to both those charges."

"Seems to be a little more serious than dogshit, Larry," Flaherty said.

Gotovich looked defensive. "Hey," he said. "It happens. Remember that family in the rent-controlled apartment? Over on Broadway? And the landlord wanted to get rid of them? So he kept doing stuff like turning off the heat and the water? And they wouldn't leave, so finally he went after them with a shotgun?"

"Yeah," Flaherty said dryly. "I remember."

I shook my head. "It's nothing like that, Larry."

"You sure?"

"Yes. I'm sure."

Before dinner that night, Jack and I traipsed around his building and up and down his street, asking all the people who were home and answering their doorbells if they'd seen anybody even remotely suspicious-looking hanging around outside his house. Nobody had. Naturally.

As we walked back to Jack's place, I said, "What did we expect?"

He snorted.

"This is a city street. Who would know who belonged here and who didn't?"

"We had to make the effort," he said, unlocking his front door.

"I know."

After dinner we sat in the living room with the list I'd compiled of all my true-crime articles. Jack had made a phone call to a connection in the Corrections Commission late that afternoon. It had paid off.

"In the past year," he said, "four of the people you wrote about at one point or another have been paroled from prison."

The list lay on the coffee table. He bent forward and tapped it with the eraser end of his pencil.

"Let me see," I said.

He pushed the list over to me. "I put a check beside each name."

I looked at the first page. Nothing there. I turned to the second page.

"Kevin Kane!" I screeched. "They let him out of prison?"

"Yup."

"My God. He was convicted on two counts of kidnapping, two counts of aggravated rape, and two counts of assault with a deadly weapon."

"Yeah, I know. But he served two-thirds of his sentence. Four years."

"Out of six," I said. "*Damn.* That infuriated me at the time. He should have gotten twenty-five years. Minimum."

"Sure," Jack said. "And he probably would have if the victim had been a Radcliffe student."

"But she was a runaway and a hooker."

"Uh-huh."

"And so that made what he did to her less of a crime." I shook my head slowly, feeling my mouth compress into a tight line. "I thought justice was supposed to be blind."

Jack didn't say anything. His silence spoke volumes.

Further down page two there was a check beside the name

of a computer genius who'd used his expertise to commit an elaborate bank fraud.

"What's this nerd doing now?"

Jack smiled. "He's renounced the world of high finance. He's working at a hospice on the Cape."

"Seriously?"

"Seriously."

"Son of a gun." I flipped to page three and scanned it. "Holy shit." Then I started to laugh.

"What?" Jack said.

"Joey DiNicola's back on the streets?"

"Live and kicking."

I continued to laugh. "Good old Joey."

Joey DiNicola was probably the most inept Mafia soldier in the entire history of organized crime, which was in fact the angle I'd used in the story I'd written about him. What was interesting was that he knew he was sort of a joke. He even enjoyed the reputation. He clowned for the press. I'd attended his racketeering trial. He was the only defendant I'd ever encountered who'd tried to use the stand as a forum for stand-up comedy. Even the judge couldn't keep a straight face. At any rate, she'd had to gavel for order a lot.

But Joey had kept his mouth shut about important company business, and served his time like a stand-up guy. So maybe he was less of a clown than he appeared.

The fourth checked-off name was that of a Boston cop who, along with three of his colleagues, had been tried for and convicted on ten counts of bribery and extortion.

"Oh, oh," I said. "Liam Lenane's out, is he?"

Jack nodded.

"What's he doing now?"

"Private security."

"I see." I chewed my lower lip, staring at the paper before

me. "Hmmm. He can't be happy about that piece I wrote about him."

Jack shrugged. "The guy's a sleazebag. Did he think that you or anyone else would blow kisses at him?"

I raised my eyebrows. "You're speaking from the standpoint of a reasonable, intelligent human being, honey. Liam isn't either of those things. Remember, he never thought he did anything wrong."

"They never do," Jack said. "That's why I think he's worth keeping an eye on."

"You think Liam wrote me those letters?"

"No," Jack said, "I don't. Not really. But out of that gang of four, he's the most likely to have."

"Mmmmm." I nodded. I glanced again at the list. "I suppose we can scratch Kevin Kane. Even though he is the most mindlessly vicious of the quartet."

"He's also an illiterate moron, honey. He can barely sign his name."

I played devil's advocate. "He could have gotten someone to write the letters for him."

"Nah, what for? He probably never even read what you wrote about him. In the first place, I doubt he can read. In the second place, nothing bad you said about him would bother him. You could call the son of a bitch a cannibal and he'd take it as a compliment."

"Okay," I said. "Scratch Kevin Kane. What about Supernerd the Computer Whiz? That piece I wrote about him wasn't exactly a puff job."

Jack frowned thoughtfully. "Good point. To me, he doesn't feel right for it, though. But I'll check some more."

I nodded. "Well, that leaves us with Joey DiNicola, and somehow, I just can't see . . ."

"Me neither."

"I mean, half the writers in Boston have done stuff on Joey. What's he going to do—send us all threatening letters?"

"Forget Joey," Jack agreed. "Whoever it is, it's not him. He'd be more likely to send you roses. He loves redheads."

I sighed, and pushed the list away from me. "Damn," I said. "Not making much headway, are we?"

"Oh, I don't know," Jack replied. "It's worth checking every possibility, no matter how . . ." His voice faded and he stared unseeingly at the wall opposite.

"What?" I said. "What are you thinking?"

He shook his head slightly. "How did the last line of the fifth letter go?"

I took a deep breath. "I'm not likely to forget. It went, 'and soon I'll come to kill you.' "

"Right."

"So?"

Jack rubbed his forehead. "So maybe whoever's writing you those letters is still in prison, but coming up for parole in a while. 'Soon I'll come to kill you.' Soon."

I frowned. "But . . . okay, I'd agree that was possible, except for one thing. How would a person in prison know that I've temporarily moved in with you?"

"He could have somebody watching you and reporting back to him."

"Jesus! Is that likely?"

"I don't know. I'm trying to cover every angle."

"Then maybe you better check the rest of the names on the list." I handed it back to him. "But is it possible for you to find out which one of those guys might be getting out of prison soon? Believe me, the corrections authorities won't tell us civilians. Particularly if us civilians happen to be writers."

"Believe me," Jack said. "I'll find a way."

*　*　*

The next day, supervised by the Cambridge Police Department armorer, I fired a gun at a target in the fifth-floor station range. He pronounced me qualified.

The thirty-eight felt heavy and cold in my hand. Very soon I'd have one just like it, my own personal deadly weapon. One the Commonwealth of Massachusetts was about to give me its permission, if not its blessing, to carry.

And, if need be, use.

I was learning that everybody had a theory about the identity of the person after me. That night I called a long-term friend, Dan Fowler, to ask if he and his companion, Steve Trask, would be interested in getting together for dinner sometime soon. He was.

"Just thought I'd let you know," I said. "I'll be bringing a gun with me to the restaurant."

There was a brief silence on the other end of the line. Then Fowler said, "Would you care to tell me why?"

"Sure." It took about five minutes.

Fowler said, "That's awful."

"Yeah."

"I'd probably pack a pistol, too, if I were you."

"Glad you understand. I promise not to threaten the waiter, though, if the service is slow."

"I wasn't really worried you would." Fowler paused. "Uh, Liz?"

"Yes?"

"You have any notion who this jerk after you might be?"

"Nope. Not really."

There was another short silence. Then Fowler said, "For what it's worth, you want my take?"

"Sure."

"It's an old boyfriend. Depend on it. You did date a crazy or two in your younger days, dear. I know. I met them."

I frowned at the receiver in my hand. "Why would he be coming out of the woodwork now?"

"Why not, if he's crazy? Who could predict what a crazy would do?"

I didn't have a quick answer to that.

3

Letter Number Six arrived at the police station the following morning. It was addressed to Jack. It said, "You can try to protect the bitch. But that won't work. Someday, when you're not looking, I'll get her."

Jack sat at his desk, the letter on the blotter before him. I sat in the visitor's chair. Flaherty was leaning with one elbow on the top of the filing cabinet.

"It could be someone who has a grudge against you," I said. "And is using me to get at you."

"Could be," Jack replied, in very even tones. He only spoke in that ultra-controlled manner when he was really raging internally.

I glanced at Flaherty. He let out a long breath and shook his head slowly. "When you getting your gun permit?"

"If all goes as it should," I said, "tomorrow."

"And not a moment too soon," he replied.

At one o'clock I had to go into Boston to interview for the second time a woman FBI agent for an article on what it was like to be the only female working for the bureau's Fugitive Squad. She was a good talker, and generous with her anecdotes and observations.

On the platform of the subway station in Government Center, while I was waiting for the Lechmere train back to Cambridge, some kind of commotion broke out behind me. I turned. A man was running directly toward me, shrieking wordlessly, waving his arms, his face stretched with rage. I leaped behind a pillar. He blew past me, screaming like one of the damned. The other people in his path lurched backward or to the side to clear a way for him. He reached the escalator and bounded up it, two steps at a time. He never ceased yelling.

He was just one of Boston's battalion of demented street people, much more harm to himself than anyone else. Still, the skin on the back of my neck stayed prickled for the length of the train ride back to Cambridge.

At three-thirty I was in Jack's office, having coffee with him. He was less wound up than he had been that morning.

"It pays to have friends who have friends on the parole board," he said.

"Oh? Why?"

"Well, I was able to find out who's getting out of the slammer in a few months. You'll be thrilled. Guess."

"I haven't a clue. Thrill me."

"Wee Willie Walters."

I almost dropped my cup of coffee. "Are you shitting me?"

"I wish I were."

"Jack, Willie has good reason not to be very fond of either one of us."

"I know."

Wee Willie Walters was six feet six inches tall and weighed three hundred pounds. He was the leader of a Jamaican gang that operated out of Boston and Cambridge. They did narcotics and firearms trafficking, extortion, prostitution, and killings. Lots of killings. They called themselves the Dog Posse.

Wee Willie had been arrested, by Jack, on a drug charge. Convicted, he'd been sent to Walpole.

He was a suspect in four ghastly murders—the odds-on favorite, in fact, to have committed them.

Willie didn't just kill people. He butchered them. Everybody knew it, and nobody could prove it.

I had written about Willie's activities prior to his incarceration. I had not had many pleasant things to say about him. Few people did.

Willie was evil, degenerate, and at least half crazy. But he was also smart.

Intelligent—and literate—enough to have written the six letters. And vengeful enough to do so.

When he made threats, he carried them out. There were four dismembered corpses to testify to that.

It also didn't take much to arouse his ire. He was supposed to have hacked up one of his girlfriends because she burned a pan of pork chops.

I gave Jack a wan smile. "You think it's dear Willie who's trying to tell us something?"

"I don't know," Jack said, "but I'm sure as hell gonna find out."

I had told Chris Cameron I'd be living with Jack until further notice. She phoned me there that evening at six.

"Been thinking about your anonymous letter writer," she said.

"Yeah? What have you concluded?"

"Maybe it's some guy you rejected."

"Ah, Chris, come on. Who do you think I am? The Cleopatra of Cambridge? The Serpent of the Charles? Anyway, when would I ever get the chance to reject anybody? I can't remember the last time somebody asked me for a date. I'm with Jack all the time. I'm chronically unavailable."

"I *know* that," she said.

"Well, then," I said. "Besides, even if I did turn down some guy who asked me out, would he really start writing hate letters to me as a result? Normal guys don't react that way, Chris."

"Uh-huh," she replied. "But I'm not talking about normal guys. I'm talking about freaks. There are a lot of them out there. As you should know, since you write about them all the time."

"I write about them," I said irritably. "I don't socialize with them."

"No, no," she replied impatiently. "I don't mean that. I'm saying that at some point you might have met a real weirdo who developed a hopeless lech for you. And because he knows he can't get you one way, he's going to get you another."

"Well," I said. "Whoever this is, he *did* write a nasty letter to Jack, too."

"Then that just adds weight to what I'm saying. Your weirdo wants Jack to know that he's going to take you away from him. *Him* being Jack. *Permanently* take you away from Jack."

"That's pretty baroque, Chris."

"Liz, your whole life is pretty baroque."

I was quiet for a few seconds. The memory of the phone conversation I'd had with Dan Fowler a few days ago floated into my mind. "This is funny," I said.

"What is?"

"I told Dan about the letters. And his immediate response was that they were from an old boyfriend."

"Could be. A freaky old boyfriend."

"That's what he said."

The gun-carry permit arrived on schedule. Jack went with me to pick up the thirty-eight at the place that supplied most of the C.P.D.'s weaponry. It felt surreal to write out a four-hundred-and-some-dollar check for a killing machine.

Jack was adamant about paying for the holster. Over my protests, he said, "Think of it as an early Christmas present."

The holster was a hip job, the kind that clips onto a belt.

I hoped all my blazers and jackets were long enough to hide it. I'd hate like hell to scare the daylights out of the receptionists at any of the magazine offices I frequented.

I tried the whole rig on in Jack's bedroom. The gun tugged at the belt and bumped awkwardly against my hip. I'd been assured I'd get used to the feeling.

Slowly I turned to look at myself in the mirror over the dresser. And stared at the reflection in disbelief.

I thought I'd look like a fool.

What I looked was dangerous.

Good.

That evening, as Jack and I were in his kitchen preparing dinner, I had an idea. Or, rather, recollected one.

"You know," I said, "my first thought, when I got the first letter, was that it was from somebody pissed off at me for either the article I wrote on child porn or the one on that Dr. Evans who raped all his old-lady patients."

Jack was standing at the counter, slicing up a London broil with an electric carving knife. He stopped carving and looked at me over his shoulder. "That's an interesting point."

I shrugged. "Well, I have in the past gotten letters from people angry at me just because I wrote about disgusting people who committed disgusting crimes. Like they thought it was my fault the crimes were committed, or something. Or that because I wrote about bad guys, that made *me* just as bad. You follow?"

"Sure." He resumed carving. "Both those articles were about the worst kind of sex crimes, too. Guaranteed to touch a nerve in some people."

"Particularly the unstable ones."

"Mmm-hmm."

I got up to get the baked potatoes from the oven and the salad from the refrigerator. "In any case," I said, "anybody can take offense at anything. Particularly a kook. My God, I've met people who didn't like me just because I was taller than they were. Practically all of them men, by the way."

Jack smiled.

I put the potatoes on a plate and began tossing the salad. "If the letter writer *is* one of my readers, then how many potential suspects do you figure we have?"

"Oh," Jack mused. "About a quarter of a million, maybe."

"None of whose names we know."

"Right."

Jack brought the meat to the table, and we sat down to eat. I served the salad. The salad had artichoke hearts in it. I love artichoke hearts. I gave myself most of them. Jack didn't notice, or if he did, he didn't say anything.

We ate mostly in silence. I didn't know what Jack was thinking about. I was thinking about Dr. Murray Evans, respected physician, occasional lecturer at the Harvard Medical School, devoted father and husband, vestryman in his Episcopal church, socialite, philanthropist, avid squash player, and sex criminal. A big handsome guy with the air of a bon vivant about him. The kind of man I automatically assume has a couple of mistresses stashed here and there.

In my article about him, I presented Evans as the Jekyll-and-Hyde figure he genuinely was. The interesting thing was how many people persisted in seeing him only as Jekyll, long after the overwhelming evidence of his pathological loathsomeness had been presented in court. As if they thought that anyone who donated to the best charities and coached Little League couldn't possibly be guilty of any crime worse than parking in a tow zone.

And what crimes Evans had committed, what trusts he had betrayed. The worm at the root of his dreadful compulsion eluded my effort to pinpoint it. Nor could any of the forensic psychiatrists I spoke to identify it. Perhaps David Epstein had come closest. "Oh, hell," Epstein had said. "Why don't we just call the son of a bitch evil?"

I liked that better than any diagnostic psychobabble.

I had used Epstein's quote in my article.

Maybe Evans himself had read what I'd written about him. And had decided to respond to the article in the form of the letters I'd received.

But how soon could he come to kill me? He was going to be in prison for a long, long time.

We finished dinner. Jack washed and dried the dishes while I made coffee.

As he was putting away the broiling pan, he said, "With regard to Dr. Evans."

I looked up from the coffee pot, a little startled. We *had* been thinking about the same thing, apparently. "What about him?"

"Didn't his wife always maintain that he was innocent?"

"Dorothy? Of course she did. She had a lot to lose if he was convicted. Like money and position. But *I* didn't send her husband to prison, Jack. The judge at his trial did."

"Sure," Jack said. "But she could be furious at you for giving the whole thing as much publicity as you did."

"Furious enough to write me letters telling me she was going to kill me?"

"Maybe she's as sick in the head as her husband, honey. What kind of woman would stay married to a man who drugged and raped eighty-year-old women?"

That night, just as we were falling asleep, there was a loud thumping noise on the front porch. Lucy, dozing on the floor in front of the bed, sprang to her feet and let out a single loud, angry bark. Then she ran out of the bedroom.

Jack leaped out of bed and grabbed his jeans.

"Stay here," he ordered.

I sat up, brushing my hair from my eyes. My skin prickled with tension.

Lucy was in the hall, still barking. Jack left the bedroom, gun in hand.

I wanted to turn on the lamp on the night table, but didn't. Why advertise my presence?

My gun was on the dresser.

I could hear, faintly, the floorboards creak under Jack's tread.

Perhaps I should get my gun. I threw back the bedclothes, a nude five-foot-ten-inch tall redhead preparing to do armed battle.

Lucy's barking subsided.

Jack came back to the bedroom. He switched on the overhead light. I stared at him.

"Goddamn raccoon," he said.

Letter Seven, like Letter Five, was delivered to me at Jack's house. It was short but not sweet. It said: "Soon, bitch. Very soon."

There was an empty office on the fourth floor of the police station, halfway between the radio room and the academy classrooms. I commandeered it for my writing shop. The office was little bigger than a broom closet, but it offered a table, a chair, and, most important, quiet. I'd lugged in a boxful of reference copies of my short stories and true-crime articles. Plus my notes and files. I was getting damned tired of carting that stuff all around Cambridge.

I went to work with a grim concentration born of my resolve not to let the son of a bitch who was after me completely disrupt my life. I had deadlines to meet and I would honor them. No matter what.

Maybe the concentration also provided inspiration. At any

rate, I found myself writing quickly and cleanly. I finished within the week the two articles I'd been working on when the letter campaign had started. I knocked off the one on the woman FBI agent first. A day later, I wrapped up a piece on a seventeen-year-old boy who killed his grandmother "to see what it felt like." Then I started work on a short story due in New York in five weeks.

Business as usual. Sort of.

Early Friday afternoon Jack called me down to his office. Actually, he called up to the radio room, and somebody from there delivered the message. I trotted downstairs.

"Finally got the test results back from the state police lab," Jack said.

I lifted my eyebrows.

"The only prints on the letters were yours and mine," he continued. "Now isn't that a big surprise?"

"What about the envelopes?"

Jack held out his hands, palms up. "Your prints, mine, Sam's, and a couple of others. Nobody's with an arrest record. Or who did military or police service."

"But that doesn't necessarily mean the letter writer *didn't* do police or military service, or have a sheet."

"Of course it doesn't. Just means whoever was smart enough to wear gloves when he, she, or it wrote the letters and addressed the envelopes and mailed them."

"Check."

"Well, did you expect otherwise?"

"No." I sighed. "That's exactly what I expected."

Jack leaned back in his chair and linked his hands behind his head. "Another thing."

"What's that?"

"None of the prosecutors in the cases you've written about has gotten any threatening mail recently. None of the witnesses for the prosecution, either."

"You asked?"

"Remember what you were saying the other night about how it was the judge who sent Dr. Evans to prison, and not you?"

"Uh-huh."

"Well?"

"Sure," I said. "If some major league bad guy is mad at me for telling his story, how much more angry would he be at the assistant district attorney who got him convicted? Or the people who testified against him? Or the judge who sentenced him?"

Jack nodded.

"But I'm the only one who's been getting letters?"

"So far, anyway."

"That doesn't tell us much, does it?"

"Nope."

When I left Jack's office, I got a cup of coffee from the C.I.D. pot and took it back up to my fourth-floor shop. My work was spread out over the desk in chaotic plenitude. I looked at it for a moment. I'd stopped writing in the middle of a paragraph. Better finish before I lost the thread.

"Hell with it," I said. I took my coffee to the window and perched on the wide sill. And stared unseeingly down at Green Street.

For every good reason I could think of to suspect one particular individual of being the letter writer, I could think of an equally good reason to exonerate him or her. And vice versa.

I'd rejected the possibility that the letter writer was one of my former students on the grounds that the last time I'd taught had been too long ago for any one of them to be seeking vengeance for a bad grade now.

But . . . maybe the D or F I'd given someone in Freshman Composition or Introduction to English Literature had, four years later, kept him, her, or it out of medical school, law school, or business school.

Maybe, with the stroke of a pen on a grade sheet, I'd wrecked somebody's career.

Of course, I hadn't *given* D's and F's, any more than I'd *given* A's and B's.

Students never saw it that way, though.

It was similarly hard for me to visualize Dorothy Evans, the rapist doctor's wife, as the letter writer. Certainly I'd written an unflattering article about her husband. So had reporters for the *Globe* and the *Herald*. And the case had been fairly well covered on the local television news.

But—of all the pieces done on Murray Evans, mine was by far the longest and most detailed. And therefore the most damaging to his reputation. And, by extension, that of his wife.

I slid off the sill and went over to the box of stories and articles. I rummaged in it till I'd found the list I'd drawn up of all the true-crime pieces I'd written in the past six years. I grabbed a lined pad from the desk and returned to the window. Then I began reading through the list. Occasionally I scribbled a note on the pad.

At the end of an hour I had a second list, this one consisting of the names of all the reporters I could recall having done major newspaper or magazine stories on the same subjects. I could think of three people who'd covered Murray Evans fairly thoroughly, and twice that number who'd done Wee Willie Walters. Two other people had done Liam Lenane, the corrupt Boston cop. A lot of the financial press had written about the bankers who'd laundered money for the mob via Joey Di-Nicola. And so on . . .

I took the list down the hall to the police academy office. The door was open, so I tapped the jamb and stuck my head into the room. Sal Lucchese, the sergeant who acted as the academy registrar, was at his desk. I smiled at him. "May I use the phone? Just for some local calls?"

"Yeah, sure, help yourself." Lucchese waved a hand at the empty desk normally used by the captain in charge of the academy. Then he went back to doing whatever it was he'd been doing when I'd interrupted him. As I walked to the captain's desk I looked to see. Polishing his badge. There wasn't an awful lot to do in the academy when a recruit class wasn't in session.

Lucchese left the office about ten minutes after I started making my calls. Which was a relief, because I wasn't sure how long I'd be on the phone, and I didn't want to try his patience. Maybe he'd run out of polish.

The first person I called was Harvey Searle at the *Herald*, who'd done stuff on Wee Willie and Liam Lenane. No, he hadn't had any threatening mail lately. Yes, he had had a menacing phone call, but that was from the ex-boyfriend of one of his girlfriends.

"How can you tell which one?" I asked. "You have more girlfriends than Julio Iglesias."

The next writer I tried, Dina Hughes, had also followed Lenane and done a piece on Murray Evans. No, no one had threatened her.

It took me an hour and a half to work through my list. Of course, I didn't succeed in getting hold of everyone I called. But the ones I did reach gave me the same answer as had Dina and Harvey.

It had become our routine for me to show up outside Jack's door at 5:00 P.M. and give him an inquiring look. That was his signal to rise, roll down his shirtsleeves, and shrug into his jacket.

This afternoon, he waved me into his office. I sat down in the visitor's chair.

"What's up?" I said.

Jack had his elbows on the desk and was looking at a piece of paper between them. "You remember your pal Alan Sturgis? Supernerd the Computer Jockey?"

"Of course."

"Well, he quit his hospice job and left the Cape."

I shrugged. "So?"

Jack looked up at me. "Apparently he left in a big hurry. The reason he gave his supervisor was that he had urgent business back in the Boston area."

"Oh?"

"The hospice director," Jack added, "said that he seemed very agitated about something. The Nerd refused to tell him what."

"I see."

We walked down to the garage in the basement, where Jack kept his car.

"Can we stop at my house?" I said. "I really should check my phone messages and mail."

"Sure."

We drove to my place. There was, miraculously, an open parking place right in front. Jack backed into it.

"I'll go up with you," he said.

I nodded. If I objected, we'd have stood on the sidewalk for the next ten minutes arguing about it.

"And you wait outside till I tell you it's safe to come in."

I rolled my eyes. "Oh, *really*, Jack. Who do you think is in there? Godzilla?"

"Just *do* it," he said, curtly.

Shaking my head, I handed over the apartment keys. He unlocked the front door. My timer had switched on the lights, and the living room was bright.

The silence was weighty.

Three-room apartments don't take long to search, especially

if you know all the places in them that a bad guy might hide. Jack did.

"Okay," he yelled.

I went inside.

The message light on my answering machine was glowing like a tiger's eye. I poked the retrieval button. Jack stood beside me as I listened to the messages. Both of us were half expecting one of them to be a threat.

Of the ten, seven were calls from various friends and acquaintances. One was a sales pitch for aluminum siding. Two were from editors asking me to write pieces for them.

I smiled at Jack. "Not a letter writer among them."

"He'd be too smart to leave a recording of his voice," Jack said. "Or *her* voice."

"Yeah."

I had gathered up my mail—all innocuous—from the box downstairs.

"I need to pick up a little fresh clothing," I said. "Why don't you make yourself a drink?"

"Nah. I'll just wait here."

"Whatever." I went into the bedroom.

Jack had switched on the bedside lamp while making his security check. Everything was as it should be, yet somehow the room and its furnishings had a faintly alien feel. Funny how that could happen to the most familiar of places uninhabited for even the briefest of times.

I pulled open my top dresser drawer.

The harsh, ragged noise I made in the back of my throat was loud enough to bring Jack running.

He burst through the bedroom doorway. "What is it?"

I pointed at the open dresser drawer.

He crossed the room and looked at what lay nestled on a pile of underwear.

"Jesus Christ," he said.

It looked like a Barbie doll. It was naked. Someone had painted a bright red cross over its chest area with what looked like nail polish.

It had long red hair. Just like mine.

4

"None of your neighbors heard or saw anything," Jack said. He rubbed his forehead, slowly and hard. It was 1:00 A.M., and he looked inexpressibly weary.

"How did he get in?" I asked. "Any ideas?"

Jack looked up at me. "Your kitchen window. The one over the deck. The lock was popped."

I closed my eyes. "Oh, Christ," I said. I shook my head.

"Let's have some booze." Jack got up and went to the cabinet for glasses. I stared blankly at the tabletop.

We were at his place, naturally. Even if I could have, I wouldn't have stayed in mine. The very air in it seemed contaminated.

"It's really stupid," I said. "But you know what makes me feel the most sick?"

"What?"

"The idea of that—whatever kind of creature he or she is—touching my underwear. Rummaging in *my* stuff. I feel like burning all of it. *Stupid.* I could be lying somewhere with my heart cut out and I'm worried about my underpants."

Jack paused on his way to the refrigerator for ice and put a hand on my shoulder. "You feel raped."

"Sort of." I dragged my hair back from my face with both hands. "I should be scared out of my wits. I mean, this joker really wants to kill me. But I'm . . ."

"What?"

"Just so *angry*?"

Jack brought the drinks to the table.

"Angry enough to kill," I added.

He nodded, then smiled faintly. "I hope you don't think you're shocking me."

"No."

We sipped our drinks.

"One good thing," I said.

"Oh, really? What's that? Tell me. I'd like to know what's good about any of this."

I pushed the corners of my mouth up in a simulacrum of a smile. "At least we can eliminate Wee Willie Walters from the suspect parade."

"We can?"

I scowled at Jack. "He's still in prison. Would they let him out early just so he could put a dead doll in my dresser drawer?"

Jack said, "The boys in his gang are loyal to him. Maybe he got one of them to do it for him, the same way he could have gotten one of them to mail you the letters. And, Liz, leave us not forget, the guy *is* a butcher."

I let out my breath softly. "Of course. An eviscerated doll would make a good trademark, wouldn't it?"

The next morning I practiced dry-firing my gun at the bedroom wall in Jack's apartment. They let me practice the real thing in the shooting range on the fifth floor of the police department that afternoon. I used up a whole box of cartridges.

The target was a drawing of a human figure. If only I'd had a face to put on it.

I scored heavily in the killing zone anyway.

The police had done their forensic thing in my apartment. As anyone could have predicted, there were no prints in the place that didn't have a perfectly safe, legal, and logical reason for being there.

The red-haired doll got sent to the state police crime lab.

*   *   *

Supernerd the Computer Jockey, aka Alan Sturgis, had family in Arlington. Jack had a friend on the police force there.

"I asked Teddy Byrne to make an inquiry for me," Jack said. "Very casually."

"And?"

"Well, Sturgis *did* have urgent business in the Boston area, like he told his boss. Only it was urgent family business. His mother had to have bypass surgery."

I pushed out my lower lip, brooding. "Okay, I can see why he'd want to come up from the Cape to be with her. But . . ."

"But what?"

I raised my right hand, then let it drop to my knee. "Why didn't he just explain the situation to the hospice director?"

Jack shrugged. "Some people don't like talking about personal stuff to their employers."

"Sure. But there's something else, too. Sturgis didn't have to quit his job. He could have asked for a leave of absence. I'm sure that under the circumstances his boss would have gladly given it to him. Especially a boss who was a hospice director. Those people above all know what it's like to deal with serious illness."

"Yeah," Jack said. "I thought of that, too."

I left his office and trudged upstairs to my own. The clutter on the desk looked almost startlingly normal. Thank God I had the writing to occupy my mind. Otherwise, I think I would have fragmented. It wasn't so much that I was scared, although I was. Or even that I was very, very angry.

I didn't like being played with this way.

It made me feel helpless.

Which, above all things, made me crazy.

On the ride home that night, Jack came up with another theory. As we were turning into his street, he said, "Come to think of it, an eviscerated doll would make a good trademark for a doctor, too. Or a doctor's wife."

"Like Dorothy Evans?" I almost smiled at the image of that face-lifted matron in ranch mink and Oriental pearls climbing through my kitchen window.

"Actually," Jack said, "it wouldn't be a bad trademark for somebody who'd worked in any kind of medical environment."

"Like a hospice?"

"Uh-huh."

After dinner, I got out a copy of the article I'd written on Alan Sturgis and reread it. As part of the background for the piece, I'd done interviews with people who'd known him in high school. The interesting thing was how little impression he'd made on any of them. He hadn't been a pariah, the way many intellectually gifted teenagers are if they haven't also been blessed with compensatory good looks and charm. Nor had he been Mr. Popularity. He certainly hadn't been a jock. He hadn't belonged to a clique. He hadn't even belonged to that last refuge of adolescent nerds, the Science Club. He hadn't had a girlfriend. He hadn't caused trouble. One guidance counselor finally recalled that he'd been awfully good at math.

His academic record at engineering school had been distinguished. Otherwise he hadn't cut a much more memorable figure there than he had in high school. "A bright young man," his advisor had told me. "No doubt about that. Extraordinary intellect. But, my lord, he was dull."

I looked at the picture of Sturgis that had run with the article. It had been taken following his arraignment, as he was leaving the court. It showed a tall, overweight young man with straw-colored lank hair and a plump-cheeked face. He wore corduroy slacks, a down parka, and round, wire-rimmed glasses. He had a slight overbite. His face was blank.

He'd shown absolutely no emotion throughout his trial. He hadn't even seemed terribly interested in the proceedings. When the jury had returned the guilty verdict, he hadn't reacted.

Did his still waters run deep? Or just murky?

Later that evening I was in Jack's basement sorting laundry and listening to a radio talk show about weird religious cults when I remembered one of the weirdest of them all: the Conventicle of Saints. I'd written about them six months ago for *New England Chronicle.*

The Conventicle had been founded by one Ray Bamford, an ex-used–car salesman originally from Indianapolis, who'd found God while doing time for insurance fraud. On his release from prison in May 1985, Bamford and his wife, Ella Mae, had relocated to Boscawen, New Hampshire. There they bought an acre of land. The trailer perched on cinder blocks that came with the land served as their home and, for lack of a better term, church offices. Ray erected a marquee behind the trailer to accommodate outdoor services. He then took out ad space in the *Manchester Union-Leader* and several smaller local papers announcing the opening of a new Christian church, one dedicated to a pure and holy way of life, as simple as that led by Jesus and His disciples.

When I'd begun my research into the Conventicle, I'd consulted with a friend of mine studying at Andover-Newton, a priest at Boston College, the Episcopal chaplain at my undergraduate school, a Methodist minister, a Conservative rabbi, and a Lutheran pastor. None of us, separately and together, were able to figure out exactly what Ray's theology was. Fundamental, evangelical, and charismatic were adjectives that applied but didn't describe. The B.C. priest probably summed it up best when he commented that Ray's devotion seemed more focused on the Sign of the Dollar than the Sign of the Cross. The Conventicle of the Saints required not a ten percent but a fifty percent tithe of its faithful. All this money, of course, subsidized the work of the Lord and not the fifteen-room house on ten acres of land that Ray and Ella Mae bought outside West Lebanon, New Hampshire, in 1987. Ray and Ella Mae also acquired, respectively, dark-blue and powder-blue Mercedes 450 SLs to ferry them to and fro on their missions of charity.

A nice income also came from their mail-order business. A tasteful catalogue featured such items as a needlepoint kit of Jesus driving the moneychangers from the Temple (@ $49.95), a Garden of Gethsemane birdbath (@ $119.95), Bibles bound in pink simulated calf, yellow simulated suede, and blue simulated alligator (each $29.95), and, naturally, framed full-color autographed photos of Ray and Ella Mae (@ $59.95). I was hoping for a Mary Magdalene matching nightie and negligee set, but no such luck.

If the Conventicle had confined itself to ripping off fools with money to burn—people who'd been Rolfed, ested, TMed, and channeled, and were now in search of the latest spiritual frisson—its existence would have been merely a bad joke. But the vast majority of Ray's adherents were those who could least afford to part with half their incomes.

And how did Ray attract them? By appealing to family values. By convincing his flock that he was the last bulwark against crime, drugs, and communism. That he alone stood between the faithful and a debauched Armageddon.

The bleakest tragedy was that most of the Conventiclers were honest, hardworking people who felt they *had* been shafted by traditional religion and politics.

I once interviewed one of Ray's—I can only think of them as victims. Too proud to accept welfare, she'd worked in a mill in Manchester to support five children after her husband had died in a construction accident while the oldest kid was still in junior high.

"I got sick of them rich liberals telling me I gotta pay higher taxes for the homeless and the colored and the Puerto Ricans," she told me. "I used to go to a church here in town. But the minister, he don't want to do nothing for us. No, it's all, we gotta help the people in, what's it down there, some South American country. I say, what about me and mine right here? I got nothing. What am I supposed to give?"

She had a point, of course. Some of *my* least favorite people were the tax-sheltered millionaire socialists who exhorted everyone of lesser means to subsidize the downtrodden while feeling no obligation to do so themselves. And despite the ugly comments the woman had made about the nonwhite and the homeless, she wasn't at bottom a bad person. She was just . . . exhausted by the desperation of her own existence. How could she show charity, having never received it?

Ray, being the truly evil person he was, took this woman's and others' legitimate complaints, shaped them, and directed them not at a screwed-up system but on some more easily objectified targets. In this respect his theology was quite simple: eliminate working women, single women, birth control, abortion, homosexuals, nonwhites, Jewish Communists, most Catholics, the income tax, and the Bill of Rights and America would once again be the Promised Land.

The other reporters and I who'd covered Ray and the Conventicle joked painfully that Ray's all-purpose villain was a black Lesbian feminist communist ACLU official who'd robbed her abortionist at gunpoint to support her drug habit.

What brought Ray to the attention of the authorities was the fact that, in addition to not believing in traditional religion or traditional politics, he didn't believe in traditional medicine, either. Many of his followers were elderly, and they suffered the various complaints of people in that age bracket: arthritis, rheumatism, high blood pressure, arteriosclerosis, congestive heart failure, and Alzheimer's. Plus cancer and MS and Huntington's chorea among the younger people as well. Ray had managed to convince a lot of these sufferers to abandon their medications and their physicians—doctors, after all, being members of a socialistic money-grubbing cabal.

Ray's therapy for the sufferers suggested first of all that they donate all the money they would ordinarily have paid for medical care and medical insurance to the Conventicle. The therapy also assured that Ray and Ella Mae would pray on behalf of the afflicted. Finally it required that the sick person spend a night in the woods, equipped only with a light blanket and a canteen of water, in strict meditation. Preferably this meditation would be performed on an inclement night in order that the flesh and spirit be properly mortified.

Ray's therapy had resulted in the deaths of seventeen people, including one eighty-seven-year-old Alzheimer's patient and one ten-year-old boy with Down's syndrome.

When the New Hampshire Attorney General's office cast a cold eye on Ray and Ella Mae and the Conventicle, so did I and a bunch of reporters from the *Boston Globe*, the *Boston Herald*, the *Manchester Union-Leader*, the *Rutland Herald*, and a host of other papers. We had a swell time with our investigations.

My principal source was a twenty-seven-year-old auto mechanic from Newport, New Hampshire. When I met Matthew Aherne he was a Conventicle drop-out. And he was more than ready to talk about what he'd heard and seen during his year and a half in Ray and Ella Mae's flock.

Matt had gone through some bad times as a teenager— expulsion from high school, a few disorderly conduct arrests, getting kicked off road crew and construction jobs for showing up for work drunk. Then he'd gotten into drugs in a big way.

Matt was screwed up, but he was fundamentally smart and decent. Bright enough, anyway, to take responsibility for his own mistakes and get himself into a rehabilitation facility after he'd hit bottom and been kicked out of the family home. Two months clean, he'd enrolled in a training program for auto repair. One year clean, he'd gotten married to a young woman named Theresa Hitchcock, a day-care worker in Dartmouth. He and Theresa now had two-year-old twins, Jason and Tiffany.

Theresa, whose childhood religious training had been fundamentalist, was the Conventicle true believer in the family. Matt, a lapsed Catholic, was skeptical of Ray's legitimacy from the start. And he absolutely drew the line at contributing fifty percent of his income to the Conventicle's coffers. But he didn't mind accompanying Theresa to the prayer meetings. As he told me with a wise-ass grin, they were a good sideshow. Especially when the sinners rose up to confess. "Man," Matt had said. "The things some of these swamp Yankees get up to. Whoo-*ee*."

But, for him, the Conventicle stopped being a laugh riot when the Alzheimer's patient and the boy with Down's syndrome died alone in the woods. Theresa too had become disenchanted. And so they'd left the flock.

When he heard I was doing a piece exposing the Conventicle, Matt had come to me. The stories he'd told had been alternately hysterically funny and sickening.

In the course of our talking, Matt and I had conceived an odd little buddyship. When he found out I'd once been a university English teacher, he was full of questions. It turned out he was thinking of taking courses at one of the local community colleges. I was happy to advise him.

Matt and Theresa weren't alone in their abandonment of the Conventicle. A good number of other devotees had fallen away in the aftermath of the deaths in the woods. Nevertheless,

Ray and Ella Mae retained a hard core of adherents who made very plain their displeasure with the godless reporters' attempts to smear the Shepherd and Shepherdess. When a guy from the *Globe* tried to interview one of Ray's deacons, he found himself staring into the double barrel of a shotgun.

My article on the Conventicle was the biggest, nastiest, and splashiest of all—purely by circumstance. Working as I was for a magazine, I had the lead time to compose a long, comprehensive piece. The newspaper people, on the other hand, had twenty-four-hour deadlines to observe, so their articles came out over the course of several weeks. Mine suffered no such dilution.

Had it enraged one of the hard-core Conventiclers so much that he or she would want to kill me?

Hadn't my reaction to the first letter been that it might be the work of a born-again cuckoo clock?

When the clean wet laundry was tumbling around in the dryer, I bounded back up the stairs to the kitchen. Jack was finishing the dinner dishes.

"What's up?" he asked.

"Give a listen," I replied.

He dried his hands on the dishtowel and joined me at the table.

"Remember that piece I did on that weirdo religious group in New Hampshire?"

"Sure."

I explained.

When I'd stopped speaking, he shook his head. "Yeah. Guess it wouldn't hurt to put Ray and Ella Mae on the suspect list, too."

"If you find me face-down drowned in a Gethsemane birdbath, you'll know for sure."

"Well, in case that happens—do you want to be buried in a Mary Magdalene negligee?"

"With a pink simulated calf Bible in my hands."
"Gotcha."

We could joke about it, but so could the letter-writer. Was it only a coincidence that Letter Number Eight arrived on October 31? The letter read: "Did you like the doll? Did it remind you of someone? The countdown is beginning."

"So what the hell does countdown mean?" I said.

I was in Jack's office, with Sam Flaherty and two other cops named Artie Lorenzo and Bobby St. Germain.

"Makes me think of the space shuttle," Lorenzo said.

I looked sideways at him. "I *don't* think I've said or written anything recently to piss off anybody at Cape Canaveral."

He smiled. "Didn't say you did."

"Seventy-two hours to lift-off," St. Germain said.

I nodded. "That would mean he's going to try to kill me three days from now. Whoopee."

"Or three days from whenever he or she sent the letter," Flaherty remarked.

"Which means tomorrow."

We were all silent for a moment.

"Ten, nine, eight, seven," I said. "Six, five, four . . ."

"Hours?" Lorenzo mused.

"It's been a lot longer than ten hours since that letter was postmarked," St. Germain said.

"Five since I received it," I said. "That means five more to go."

Jack shook his head. "The sender wouldn't be able to calculate that. Mail gets delivered any time between eleven and two, in my part of town."

"Well," I said lightly, "stick by me, anyway, for the rest of today and tonight, big boy. I may not be able to get to my gun in time."

"Don't worry," Jack said. "I give good back-up."

St. Germain snickered.

"Days," Lorenzo said. "Ten days."

Jack nodded. "Yeah, that's it, most likely. We know it's not minutes. And it probably isn't weeks or months. Certainly not years."

"Ten days from yesterday or today?" I asked.

"Let's assume both," Jack said. He leaned backward in his chair, tapping his chin with a pencil. "Hell, we don't even know that he's counting down from ten."

"Could be fifteen," St. Germain said. "Or twenty."

"Whatever," Flaherty said. "Happy Halloween."

On the way out of Jack's office, Lorenzo gave me a light little punch on the upper right arm.

"Hey," he said. "You got a lot of spirit, you know? I like that."

"Thanks."

"I mean, the way you can kid around about this shit."

"Artie," I said, "that's unfortunately all I *can* do."

"Yeah," he said. "Tell me about it."

Later that day I called Matt Aherne at the West Lebanon Porsche-Audi dealership where he was head mechanic.

"Liz," he said. "How ya doin'? When you coming up for a visit?"

"Soon, I hope. How are you?"

"Good, real good."

"And Terry and the kids?"

"Oh, they're great. Listen, what's up?"

I sighed. "I'm not sure, Matt. Can I ask you a strange question?"

He laughed. "Yeah, sure."

"Have you been threatened recently?"

"*What?*"

I explained.

"Jesus," he said when I'd finished. His voice was slow and very troubled. "Jesus. No, Liz, I haven't heard one word from anybody in the Conventicle. Terry neither."

"I'm glad."

"You really think one of Ray's nutcakes could be after you?"

"I don't know. Remember how one of them pointed a shotgun at the *Globe* reporter?"

"Yeah, yeah," Matt said. "Deacon Strong."

"Right."

"Liz?"

"Yes?"

"Why do you think anybody from the Conventicle would wanna get me? I mean, like it wasn't me that wrote the article."

"Sure, Matt," I said. "But you were my chief source. And you went on the record with some very damaging stories about them. They could feel that you, oh, betrayed them. One of the real far-out nuts might want to get you to prove his loyalty to Ray and Ella Mae."

"I'd like to see somebody try."

"Well, be that as it may—you *will* be careful, won't you? Keep an eye out?"

"Yeah, sure. You too, Liz."

"I will. And Matt—"

"Yeah?"

"Let me know if you get a funny letter or phone call, okay?"

"Yeah, sure."

"All right. Give my love to Terry and the kids."

"Yup. Oh, hey, Liz? You know? I started two courses at night school this September."

"Matt! That's wonderful. What are you taking?"

"Survey of American Lit and Intro to American History."

"My *man*. That's terrific. How are you liking them?"

"Oh, they're all right, you know? Reading load's a little heavy, but nothing I can't handle, you know?"

"I know. That's great, Matt."

"I gotta tell you one thing, though."

"What's that?"

"I can't deal with that friggin' *Moby-Dick*."

"Matt?"

"Yeah?"

"Neither could I."

"You shitting me? You used to be a professor."

"Doesn't mean I loved everything I ever read. Or even that I read it all the way through."

He laughed. "Listen, Liz, I got a Porsche here with a cracked engine block."

"Then by all means give it your best attention," I said. "I won't keep you."

I gave him Jack's home phone number. And told him to call me there any time.

What a doll he was. I felt better about whatever little help I'd given him than practically any of my other so-called *real* students.

If someone from the Conventicle *was* after me, I was certain it wouldn't be Ray Bamford himself, nor Ella Mae. One of their nutcakes, to use Matt's word. And not necessarily one acting on his or her own. Either Ray or Ella Mae could have ordered some fanatic to harass and finally kill me. And be completely certain that the order would be obeyed. To the letter.

I had tried and failed repeatedly to interview Ray and Ella Mae. The *Globe* and *Herald* reporters and I had even snuck into one of the prayer meetings, been discovered halfway through, and ejected by two of the burlier deacons (not the shotgun-wielding one). Even so, I'd been able to form distinct impressions of the Bamfords.

Sleaze incarnate.

Ray was tall and thin, with very pale skin and black hair swept straight back from a high forehead. His nose was beaklike and his chin prominent. And he smiled. Oh, how he smiled.

Ella Mae was short and tubby with a moon face and the bee-stung lips and huge eyes of Betty Boop. Her hair was dyed a midnight shade so black it was almost navy.

She and Ray sat side by side on a raised platform in the huge converted barn that now housed the services. They dressed identically in flowing white caftans.

Like Ray, Ella smiled a lot. Except when a sinner rose to confess. Then she wept. Without wrecking her makeup. Either her mascara was titanium-based or she'd had her eyelashes tinted to match her hair.

When Ray wasn't wrestling with Satan for dominion over the souls of the backsliders in his congregation, he was sermonizing. The subject of the sermon the day the two reporters and I attended was the inherent evil of the elderly unmarried working woman. Elderly turned out to mean over eighteen. The *Globe* and *Herald* reporters, who happened to be male, couldn't keep straight faces. Harvey Searle from the *Herald* kept glancing at me out of the corner of his eyes and breaking down into helpless giggles.

I thought it was funny, too, but not quite as comic as the two guys did.

Unfortunately we got bounced from the meeting before we heard what Ray's solution to the problem of career she-devils might be.

Line 'em up and shoot 'em?

In that case, I was at least equipped to shoot back.

Letter Number Nine arrived the next day. Except it wasn't a letter. It was a photograph of me, the standard one that accompanied some of my magazine articles. It had been clipped from a glossy.

Where my eyes should have been were little charred holes, as if someone had held the tip of a lit cigarette to them.

"You recognize what magazine this came from?" Jack asked.

I nodded. "The issue of *Cambridge Monthly* that ran my article about Dr. Evans. Some of the article text is on the reverse side of the picture."

"Uh-huh," Jack said. He poked the transparent plastic evidence folder into which the cut-out photo had been slipped. "I think it's about time I got in touch with the Wellesley police and asked them to do a little discreet checking up on Dorothy Evans."

"I suppose it is," I said.

We looked at the evidence folder. In our minds was the same thought.

Murray Evans had been an ophthalmologist. He had done laser surgery on a lot of eyes.

I got up in the middle of the night to go to the bathroom. Jack wasn't in the bed beside me. The light was on in the kitchen. Curious, I shuffled out there, rubbing my eyes and blinking.

Jack, fully dressed, was at the table, a cup of something before him.

"What're you doing?" I said. I peered at the clock. It was 3:00 A.M.

He shrugged, and ran a hand back through his thick, gray-tinged brown hair. "Couldn't sleep." He turned the cup around on the table.

I pulled out a chair and sat down opposite him. "What are you drinking?"

"Tea. Want some?"

I shook my head.

He smiled slightly. "Why don't you go back to bed? You look worn out."

So did he. "I will if you'll come with me."

"I'll be along in a while."

I gazed at him for a moment. "You're doing guard duty, aren't you?"

He shrugged again. "I was awake anyway. Why not?"

"Oh, Jack."

He made a quick dismissive gesture with his right hand. I sighed. Then I got up and walked around the table to where he was sitting. I bent down and laid my cheek against the top of his head, sliding my arms around him.

"You know, honey," I said, "I hope you don't plan on doing this every night until the person either stops writing me letters or . . . we find out who it is."

"I will if I have to," he said.

The next afternoon, I went down to Jack's office to find out if he'd heard anything from the Wellesley police about Dorothy Evans. He had a visitor—a six-foot-tall, slim, strikingly beautiful black woman. She grinned at me in greeting.

"Cassie," I said, startled. "Hi. Haven't seen you in ages."

Cassandra Stewart was an assistant district attorney for Middlesex County. She and Jack had worked a number of cases together over the years. I'd written up some of them.

"Pull up a chair," Jack said.

I took the one beside the filing cabinet and hitched it up alongside the desk.

"What's happening?" I said.

Jack and Cassie glanced at each other.

"It's your story," Jack said.

Cassie leaned back and smoothed her gray wool suit skirt over her thighs.

"The night before last," she said, "I got your basic menacing phone call."

"Oh?"

"Yes, a gentleman informing me that my days are numbered."

"Those were his words?"

"No, actually what he said was, 'Bitch, your sweet nigger ass is dead real soon.'"

I grimaced. "Lovely. Did you recognize the voice?"

She shook her head. The big silver hoops in her earlobes danced.

The office was silent.

Jack and Cassie looked at me.

"Christ," I said. "You were the prosecutor in the Wee Willie Walters case."

5

A week passed, during which I received no more letters or scorched photographs. And no one had so far broken into either my place or Jack's to leave a second dead red-haired doll in a dresser drawer.

I was still living with Jack, though, and still parked in my police station writing workshop. The only difference was that I'd taken the gun off my hip, at least when I was at Jack's or at the P.D. I'd very quickly started feeling like a horse's ass strolling around the station wearing it. Like I was pretending to be a cop or something.

I had a big purse with a compartment in it that accommodated the gun nicely.

But I hadn't let down my guard. Just because the letter-writer had seemingly gone into hiatus didn't mean he'd called it quits altogether. Maybe he was just psyching himself up for his next big move. Whatever *that* might be.

I *did* wear the gun when I went out, even if it was only to the library or the post office or some magazine's editorial offices. And of course I wore it on the subway or the bus. Anybody who tried to mug me was going to get a *giant* surprise.

I'd grown accustomed to the presence of the gun in my life. I wondered if the day would ever come when I'd start thinking of it as just another personal appliance, like my hot rollers or blow dryer or toothbrush.

Like hell.

Another thing I'd grown accustomed to was living with Jack.

That surprised me a little. I loved him to death, and I had no desire to screw around (there was nothing better than him out there anyway) and I hoped we'd be together for the rest of our lives. But something in me resisted making that final leap into living together permanently or getting married. It wasn't a feminist objection—and I was raised to be a feminist. I was strongly in favor of marriage and family. If *they* didn't exist, *I* wouldn't exist.

It was temperament, I guess. I think I'm fundamentally a loner. Jack is, too, but in a slightly different way. He was married once. He probably still would be, to the same woman, if she hadn't been killed by a drunk driver three years before I'd met him.

We didn't talk about our future together much. I shied away from the subject. He, sensing that, didn't raise it. That made me feel bad, sometimes. I had the idea he'd like to be married and have kids. Was I depriving him of that chance?

The rational side of me said that if he *really* wanted to start a family, he could break with me and find another woman. A younger one, more flexible than me in every way.

But he didn't. And he didn't pressure me. So we both let it ride. I salved my conscience with the reminder that what he and I had together was outstanding.

I was still working on the short story I'd begun before the arrival of the doll and the burned-eyes photo. It wasn't going well. Maybe I was still too tense about the letter writer to relax enough to be creative. The story was due in New York by Thanksgiving. I had never missed a deadline and I didn't intend to start now.

Normally I like writing short stories. The problems and challenges are different from those posed by nonfiction. For one thing, you have to worry about a plot. And you also have to worry about character development. With a true-crime article, you got plot and character served to you on a plate.

I'd published about four pieces of fiction over the past few years. I was about a third of the way through of the story I was working on now. And stuck there. Plot difficulties. I knew what the end of the story would be; I just couldn't quite figure out how to get to it.

I'd gotten over the hump four times in the past, so presumably I could do so a fifth. Maybe if I looked at how I'd made the leap then, I'd get inspired about a way to do it now.

I picked up a copy of the magazine that had run my first story and flipped through it. I practically never reread my old fiction. On the rare occasions when I did, I had to grit my teeth. All I could see was what was wrong with it. Oddly, I never reacted that way to my true-crime stuff.

I tossed the first magazine aside and picked up a second. The story here was a short-short, more of a set piece than anything else. I skimmed the last few paragraphs, and wondered why an editor had paid me money for it.

The third story was much longer. It also made me even more uncomfortable than the others. The main character was a very thinly disguised version of a guy I'd been involved with about a year before I'd met Jack. The affair had ended badly. Very badly. What I'd written about it had been as much a ritual of exorcism as a vehicle of revenge.

I braced myself and began reading. This would be the first time I'd looked at the story since it had been published.

I was surprised to find the piece . . . not awful. The portrayal of Garrett in all his psychotic splendor was actually pretty good. At least it wasn't a caricature, as in retrospect I had feared it would be.

Still, there weren't any clues in the story as to how to solve my present case of writer's block. I finished it, set it aside, and reached for number four.

I had skimmed halfway through number four when the real significance of number three struck me. I let the magazine drop to my lap. It slithered to the floor in a rustle of high-gloss paper.

I'd been operating on the assumption that whoever had written me the letters and put the doll in my dresser was probably someone I'd written about.

In a true-crime piece.

It literally, genuinely, honestly had never occurred to me until this very moment that any *fiction* of mine might make anyone insane enough with rage to want to kill me.

Of course, all my fictional characters were inventions.

With the dazzling exception of Garrett Hibley. Called Gerard Harris in the story I'd written about him.

I ran down the cast-iron staircase to the third floor and blew through the double doors to the Criminal Investigation Division. The door to Jack's office was open. The office itself was empty. Marjorie, the secretary, was reading the *Herald*. She looked up from the comics and smiled at me.

"Where's Lieutenant Lingemann?" I said.

She blinked at my curt breathlessness. "On the street."

"Do you know when he'll be back?"

"Oh." She frowned. "Maybe . . . a quarter to five? Like that?"

I must have looked disappointed, or disturbed, by the reply, because she added, "You want, we can call him in. If it's important."

I sucked in my lower lip and clamped it between my teeth. Then I shook my head. "No. Never mind."

She frowned. "Sure?"

I hesitated a second. "No. It's okay."

Marjorie looked across the room. "Detective Buchanan is here. Could he help you?"

I shook my head again. I didn't want to discuss this with

anyone but Jack, at least to begin with. "It can wait. Thanks."
I smiled at her mechanically. She nodded and went back to
the paper. I left the C.I.D.

The rush of revelation is like what I've heard about a cocaine
rush—it dissipates in ten minutes. The difference between the
two is that the aftermath of the drug high leaves you depressed
and the aftermath of the revelation high leaves you thoughtful.
I got myself a cup of coffee from the pot in the academy office
and returned to my cubbyhole. I sat down, leaning back in
the chair and putting my feet on the desk.

What I had to do was consider, as calmly and logically as
possible, the idea that Garrett Hibley had sent me eight threatening letters, a mutilated photograph, and left an eviscerated
Barbie doll in my dresser drawer. And was planning to come
and kill me in the very near future.

The refrain that rang in my brain was, *Well, the son of a
bitch is just sick enough to do just that, isn't he?*

Still crazy after all these years. Seven of them, to be exact.

He would hate me for having written about him. He'd hated
me anyway, at the end.

But . . . why had he waited until now to work himself into
such a fury over my fictional representation of him and our
affair? The story had been published five years ago.

Maybe he'd only run across it recently. Maybe someone
who knew us both had pointed it out to him. And made a
snide comment.

And would that set him off? Yes, it would. Lesser things
had. That much I could confirm from my own experience.

Goddamn it, it *was* Garrett. It had to be Garrett.

I looked at my watch: two-thirty. Garrett would be at work
now. When I'd last known him, he'd been a rising star in the
research lab of a Cambridge bioengineering firm. I had no
reason to think he wouldn't still be there. They'd loved him.

I grabbed the phone book and flipped it open to H. There

was a listing for a G. Hibley at a Cambridge address, not the one he'd lived at when we'd been together. I copied it and the phone number down on a scrap of paper. For future reference, if necessary. Maybe I could start sending *him* threatening mail.

The anger inside me was a glowing filament ready to burst into flame.

I reached for my shoulder bag. The gun was there, in an inner compartment. I knew it would be; it always was. Looking at it made me feel cold and hard and resolved.

I swung my feet to the floor with a loud thump.

Do it.

Bioline of Cambridge was on Binney Street between Kendall Square and the courthouse. The lobby looked more like that of a small three-star hotel than of a business operation. The carpeting was pale-green plush (the cleaning bill for it must have been humongous) and the walls white, decorated with blown-up color photographs of DNA molecules and other less readily identifiable organisms. There was a small kidney-shaped pond in which swam goldfish and other more exotic breeds. A tall, full ficus hung over it. The piped-in music was Mozart, not Muzak. A receptionist sat at a white crescent-shaped desk. Less visible was the security guard at a corner station. He was armed. That made two of us.

The receptionist was in his early twenties and clad in jeans and a plaid flannel shirt, and would have been an anomaly almost anywhere but Bioline of Cambridge. He was probably a graduate student in chemical engineering and this his part-time job. He was reading a copy of *Byte*. I smiled at him as I approached the desk.

"Is Garrett Hibley in?"

The young man squinted at me and put down the magazine. "Dr. Hibley?"

"Yes."

"Not here."

"Oh. Well, will he be back this afternoon sometime?"

The kid gave me an odd look. "I mean he's not here. Doesn't work here any more."

"Oh."

"Left about, oh, maybe a month ago."

I nodded. "I see."

The kid reached for his magazine. I bit my lower lip. "Is Denise Amaral in?"

The kid put down the magazine. "I can check." He said it as if it were a question.

"Please."

He picked up the phone receiver and punched a button on the switchboard console.

"Tell her it's Liz Connors."

The kid spoke into the phone. After a little pause, he put the receiver back on the console. "You can go up," he said. "Room Ten. Third Floor. Take the stairs or"—he jerked his left thumb over his shoulder—"the elevator."

"Thanks."

I took the stairs, partly to have the extra time for thought and partly just to look the whole building over again, after seven years. I had been here frequently when I'd known Garrett, to meet him for lunch, to meet him after work, and to be his date at office parties.

The place hadn't changed. On each floor there was a big open area with couches and chairs and coffee tables. On the tables were scattered magazines—*Scientific American*, *Omni*, *The New Yorker*, and *Mad*. The company founder firmly believed that there should be somewhere his test-tube jockeys and numbers crunchers could go to relax between big ideas and big deals. I'd sat in these lounges myself, many a time, waiting for Garrett.

Room Ten on the third floor had a sign on it that read, "D. Amaral, Ph.D. Director/Research and Development."

Denise had moved up in the hierarchy. I tapped on the door and pushed it open when someone yelled, "Come in."

The voice belonged to Denise herself. She was standing by a wall-to-ceiling bookcase, in the act of sliding a volume back onto the middle shelf.

"Liz Connors," she said. "My God. How long has it been? No, don't tell me." She crossed the room, her right hand extended. "I read stuff by you all the time."

I smiled. "Congratulations on your promotion."

She returned the smile. "Nice to see you again." She glanced over her shoulder at the far left corner of the room, where three canvas and beechwood director's chairs were grouped around a low circular table. "Sit down. Tell me what's new."

She was a sturdily built woman of middle height, wearing an unbuttoned white lab coat over a tan wool skirt and white blouse. The last time I'd seen her, her hair had been light brown. It had since been tinted to approximate the color of her eyes, a goldish hazel.

There was a coffeemaker on the window ledge. "You still a caffeine addict?" Denise asked.

"Of course."

She smiled. "Me, too. Though I've cut down a lot." She poured coffee into two trigger-handled Bennington Pottery mugs and handed one to me.

I had met Denise Amaral when she'd been one of the lab researchers working alongside Garrett. The occasion was the first Bioline office party I'd attended as Garrett's guest. Things were whooping along in a sedate way when Garrett had been paged for a phone call. I was standing by myself at the drink table, raptly observing scientific genius at play, when a young woman in jeans and an M.I.T. sweatshirt who looked vaguely familiar had come up to me and said, "You're Garrett's friend, aren't you?"

"Yes." I looked at her closely. "I've seen you before, haven't I?"

"In the lab, probably." She held out her hand. "Denise Amaral."

"Liz Connors. Are you going to have some punch?"

She made a face. "Gawd, no. Stuff tastes like a failed experiment."

I laughed, and held up my glass of vodka and tonic to show her that I agreed.

Garrett stayed away on his phone call for half an hour. I spent that time talking to Denise. She had a doctorate in microbiology from M.I.T., I learned, and had grown up in East Cambridge, the oldest daughter of Portuguese immigrants. She was the veteran of a failed graduate school marriage to another microbiology student. She lived by herself now, in an apartment five minutes from work and three blocks from the family home.

A friendship had been conceived in the conversation—a friendship that lasted as long as my affair with Garrett. After the bust-up, Denise and I had gradually fallen out of touch with each other. My doing, mostly. I hadn't wanted to be around anyone who reminded me of Garrett. No matter who they were, or how nice they'd been, they became, in my eyes, somehow tainted by the association with him.

Denise stirred powdered dairy creamer into her coffee and sat down in the director's chair opposite me, crossing her legs. I noticed a gold band on the ring finger of her left hand.

"You got married."

"Two years ago." She smiled. "He's a lawyer, not a scientist. And"—she put her left hand on her stomach—"I'm six weeks pregnant."

I raised my coffee cup. "Congratulations again."

"Thanks." She settled back in her chair. "So, what brings you here? You doing research for an article on biotech?"

I shook my head. "No. Actually, I was looking for Garrett."

She stared at me for a few seconds, then set her mug down on the table between us. "What the hell for? Why would you want to see *him*?"

I told her the whole story. Then I showed her the copies of the letters. She read them twice, the first time quickly and the second slowly, as if looking for something.

She refolded the papers. Then she rose and went to the window. She stood there a moment, staring out at Binney Street, hitting the glass gently and rhythmically with the photocopies.

The room was palpably quiet.

Denise turned to face me, leaning her hips against the windowsill.

"You really think Garrett wrote these?" she asked. "And put the doll in your dresser drawer?"

"Yes. I really do. You think I'm crazy?"

"No," she said. "I think you're right."

She poured me more coffee and returned to her chair.

"If Garrett had been here today," she said, "what would you have done?"

"Confronted him."

"And you weren't afraid of what he might do if you did?"

I opened my purse and held it out to show her the contents.

Her eyes widened. "My God. Do you have a license for that?"

"Yes."

She nodded, and inhaled deeply through her nose, her mouth a narrow tight line.

"But," I said, "the reason I chose to confront him here was precisely because I knew it would be pretty safe. I mean, he wouldn't try to stab or strangle me in a lab surrounded by other people, would he? And even if he did go crazy and try something, the others there would stop him."

"I suppose."

"The gun's a last resort. I don't want to shoot the son of a bitch. I want to see him arrested. By Jack, my friend on the cops."

Denise sighed. "For someone with Garrett's ego, that would be worse than being shot."

I smiled. "Exactly."

She eyed me. "You're pretty cool about this."

I shook my head. "No, not really. I'm boiling inside. I'm just keeping a lid on it."

"I see."

I stretched out my legs. "The kid down in the reception area said that Garrett left here about a month ago. Where'd he go?"

"Kendall Associates."

"They make him an offer?"

Denise nodded. "Huge. There was really no way we could top it. But . . ." She made a vague movement with her left hand. "We wouldn't have tried, either."

"Oh?"

"No. Actually"—she took another deep breath—"we were glad to see him go."

"The boy wonder?"

She nodded. "There were difficulties."

"Can you specify?"

She gave me a very direct look. "One of the women in the lab was about to bring a sexual harassment suit against him."

I raised my eyebrows. "Somehow, that doesn't surprise me."

"I guess it wouldn't. There were other problems, too."

"Like what?"

"Well, there was a huge blow-up between Garrett and one

of the other guys on his project team. Garrett was convinced this guy was trying to steal some of his private research."

"And was he?"

Denise snorted. "No, of course not."

"Garrett always was a little paranoid about things like that."

"The tendency's gotten worse in recent years."

"Uh-huh." I finished my coffee. "Denise, I've heard of Kendall Associates, but I'm not exactly sure what they do."

She frowned, thoughtfully. "They're not direct competitors of ours. They do some of what we do, but also some defense stuff, which we don't, and also some subcontracting for NASA, and—"

"Jesus," I said. "NASA."

"What's wrong?"

I picked up the letters from the table and riffled through them to Number Eight. I held it up for Denise to read: "Did you like the doll? Did it remind you of someone? The countdown is beginning."

Denise looked at me with enlarged eyes.

"The expression's a common one," I said. "It could be a coincidence. But I'm betting it's not."

Denise straightened her shoulders. "I'll look back through my files this afternoon. See if I can find anything from Garrett that would give us a sample of his printing."

I snapped a thumbnail against the paper in my hand. "I'm sure he's disguised it."

She shrugged. "Worth a try."

"Sure."

"*You* don't have any samples of his writing, still, do you?"

I laughed. "Denise, any note or letter I ever got from Garrett—other than these—I burned seven years ago."

"Of course." She sighed. "Would you like more coffee?"

"No, thanks. I should be getting along. I appreciate your help, Denise."

She smiled slightly. "It was lovely to see you again. I'm sorry we didn't stay in touch. But . . . it would have been awkward, wouldn't it?"

"Yeah." I rose, and slipped into my jacket. "Good luck with the baby. You thought of a name yet?"

"We're vacillating between Alpha Interferon and Civil Procedure."

I laughed.

She held out her hand, and we shook.

At the door, I said, "Denise?"

"Yes?"

"Why were you so quick to agree with me that it's Garrett who's writing me those letters?"

She was silent for a moment. Then she said, "Because I think there's something wrong with him that's been getting progressively worse."

"Mentally wrong?"

"Yes."

I nodded. "I know that. I've always known that."

She looked at me. "It was bad, wasn't it?"

"Very."

She studied my face. "Be careful," she said. "You have no idea how much he may still hate you."

"I don't get it," Jack said. "I really don't get it. You're an attractive woman. You're intelligent. So why the hell would you want to waste a year of your life on a loser like Hibley?"

It was that evening, and I was sitting with Jack in his living room, trying to explain to him what I'd seen in Garrett. Clearly, I wasn't explaining very well. Either that, or it was inexplicable.

I sipped my drink. "He was smart, interesting, funny, and good-looking," I said. "Aren't those good reasons?"

"Liz, from what you've told me, he was also crazy."

I shook my head impatiently. "But Jack, I didn't *know* that till the end. He kept it hidden."

"No hints whatsoever?"

I thought for a moment. "No. Not really."

"What does *not really* mean?"

I sighed. "Oh, God. Let's see. Okay, the guy was—is—a scientific genius, right? And he's pretty egotistical. No, *very* egotistical. So he had a few eccentricities. I just figured they were part of the package. We all have our quirks."

"And what were his?"

I felt as if I were testifying before a grand jury and being questioned by an unusually aggressive prosecutor. "Garrett's quirks," I said. My mind went back to the conversation I'd had earlier with Denise Amaral. "Well, he was sort of paranoid."

"About what?"

"About people trying to steal his ideas."

"Uh-huh. Anything else?"

I shrugged. "That's it, really."

"Okay. Now, you say he was crazy when you two broke up. What happened? Did he suddenly go off the wall one day or night, or what?"

I shifted around on the couch, a little uncomfortably. "Well, yeah, that *is* pretty much what happened."

"Pretty much?"

"Jesus, honey, will you stop jumping on everything I say?"

"What do you mean by *pretty much*?"

I took another sip of my martini. Jack's glass of bourbon was on the coffee table, untouched. He was at the other end of the couch, sitting angled around on the edge of the cushion so he could see me directly. He was leaning forward, his elbows on his knees, watching my face very intently.

"All right, all right," I said. "A few weeks before we broke up, he started acting a little . . . well, different."

"Different how?"

I ran my index finger along the rim of my glass. "Oh—a little distant."

Jack nodded.

"I figured he was preoccupied by work. That maybe he was at a critical stage in an important project."

"Did he tell you that?"

I shook my head. "No. I asked him. He said he wasn't."

"Okay. Go on."

"Then, very occasionally, I'd get what seemed like a little flash of hostility from him." I paused. "*Hostility* may be too strong a word. Anger? Oh, hell, I don't know. It was there, though, whatever it was."

"What form did this hostility take?"

I frowned. "Oh, little verbal jabs and needles."

"Like what?"

"Oh, Jack. I can't remember word for word. It was so long ago. Just zingers. Like he'd kid me about being an up-and-coming literary star, but it would have an edge to it, you know?"

He nodded again. "Were you an up-and-coming literary star, at that point?"

I smiled. "That's a huge exaggeration. I had just had my very first two articles accepted for publication. I was walking on air."

He returned my smile. "I'm sure you were. But Hibley wasn't too happy about it."

"He *said* he was. Happy for me, I mean."

"Uh-huh. Okay, tell me about when you broke up. The night he went off the wall. It *was* at night?"

I nodded.

"Let's hear it."

I was silent.

"Liz."

I put my drink on the coffee table and crossed my arms over my chest.

"Hard to talk about?" Jack said.

I nodded again.

"It's important that you tell me."

"I know." I uncrossed my arms and reached for my drink. "Oh, God. I still get the shivers even thinking about it."

"Take your time."

I took a gulp of martini to brace myself. "It was a Friday night. I'd invited him over to dinner. It was a special meal, to celebrate that my articles were going to be published."

"Uh-huh."

"Well, he turned up when he said he would, at six-thirty, with a bottle of nice wine. But the minute he walked in the door, I could tell something was wrong."

"How?"

I shook my head. "I don't know. I could just sense a real strong tension. We had a pre-dinner drink. I tried to get a conversation going, but all I got was either monosyllabic answers or nothing at all. And we'd never had any trouble thinking of things to say to each other before then."

"Mmm-hmm."

"Okay. Well, dinner, if anything, was even worse. I could barely eat and neither could he. It was as if there were a corpse in the middle of the table instead of bowls and plates of food."

"So?"

"So I made coffee, and we went to the living room, and I got up my nerve, and I asked him what was bugging him. And he said that he didn't want to see me any more."

"Go on."

I took another sip of my drink. "I was shocked. I mean, I was really knocked out. So I just blurted, 'Why the hell not?' "

"And?"

I took a deep breath. "He told me it was because he was getting too attached to me."

Jack said, "What?"

I laughed dryly. "Yeah, I know. That was my reaction."

Jack shook his head.

"Well," I said, "I got really upset. And we went back and forth on this, and all I could get out of him was this insistence that he couldn't be involved with a woman that he really cared about. It was crazy. It made no sense. I guess . . . I started to cry. I mean, I could imagine being rejected by somebody because he decided you were boring or dumb or ugly or something, but to reject somebody because you loved them? How are you supposed to respond to that?"

Jack was silent.

I looked at him. "This next part is . . . it's really embarrassing to tell."

"Trust me; I won't blush."

I nodded. "Okay, well, what I did was, I, uh, tried to seduce him."

"Uh-huh."

I squirmed against the couch cushions. "And, uh, I got him to the bedroom, and we—you know—but he . . . oh, God. He couldn't, uh, function."

Jack's face was impassive.

"Then the really bad stuff happened," I said.

"Did he hurt you?"

"Physically? No. It was what he said. It was just . . . it was horrible. He just turned on me and ripped me apart. Everything about me. Please don't ask me to repeat any of it."

"Okay."

"He was wild, Jack. He didn't even look like himself. It was terrifying."

"And?"

"The last thing he said to me was that I was never to speak to him again. If I ever saw him on the street, or in a shop, or like that, I was to turn and start walking in the opposite direction. You see what I mean about loonie?"

"Did he threaten you?"

"Implicitly, I suppose."

"Go on."

I shrugged. "That was it. He left. I never spoke to him again." I finished my drink. "I really think he would have liked to have killed me, though."

Jack picked up his bourbon and leaned back on the couch.

"Now you know," I said.

"Now I know."

I got up and went to the kitchen to make a second drink. When I came back, Jack had his hands behind his head and his feet on the coffee table and was staring at the fireplace.

"Liz?"

"Yes?"

"IIow true to life was the story you wrote about Hibley?"

"Very."

"You're sure he'd recognize himself in it, if he read it?"

"Positive."

"Okay. You have a copy around I can see?"

"Sure, in my briefcase in the bedroom. I'll get it."

"No hurry." He reached up and took hold of my free hand. "Here, come and sit beside me a minute."

I smiled, and put my knee on the couch.

The window behind it shattered and the drapery jerked.

"Jesus Christ," Jack said. He yanked my arm and I fell forward awkwardly into his lap. Together we rolled onto the floor, him on top of me.

Another window pane imploded. The glass over a picture on the opposite wall disintegrated. Jack pressed my face into the carpet. I couldn't breathe.

The room settled into silence.

"Stay flat," Jack hissed into my ear. He lifted himself off me. I turned my head to see what he was doing. He crawled to the phone on the table in the corner and knocked it off the stand. He dialed three numbers.

"Nine millimeter automatic," the night captain said. "Found the shells in the gutter in front of the house. Two of 'em."

"Right," Jack said flatly.

The captain looked at me. "Maybe you should think about getting into another line of work. Something safe, like coal mining or testing fighter planes."

"It's a temptation," I said.

"We can put on some more extra patrols in this neighborhood," the captain said. "One of the Delta units will stay here the rest of the night."

Jack shrugged. "Whoever the shooter was, he or she's long gone."

"Sure."

"Thanks, though."

The captain smiled. "No problem."

The cops finally left around nine, except for the two in the unmarked Delta unit car. Jack nailed some thin plywood over the two broken windows.

He dropped the hammer onto the couch and turned to me, shaking his head.

"Sure do lead an exciting life, don't we?" I said.

He gave a little snorting laugh, came over to me, and looped an arm around my shoulders. I put mine around his waist.

"We never had dinner," I said. "Want to fix something with me?"

"Why not?"

"How about tunafish salad on toasted pumpernickel?"

"Sounds good."

"Okay. You do the toast and I'll do the tuna."

We went to the kitchen.

"You know," I said, "I never got to drink my second drink. I threw it across the living room when you hurled me on the floor and jumped on top of me. Guess I'll have another."

"You're entitled."

"Join me?"

"Yup."

I looked at my hands. They were rock-steady. "Jeez," I said. "You'd think I'd be shaking."

Jack was getting the bourbon and vodka from the cabinet. "Churchill," he said.

I was hunting for a can of tuna. "Hmm?"

"Didn't Churchill say something about there being nothing so exhilarating as being shot at without result?"

"Well, it wasn't Dr. Ruth." I got out a mixing bowl.

Jack handed me my drink. "Here's to being shot at without result."

We clicked glasses.

We ate the sandwiches at the kitchen table, without much conversation. Lucy lay on the floor between us, watching for a stray crust or crumb to drop. The whole shooting incident had never occurred, as far as she was concerned. She'd been snoozing on the bedroom floor when it happened.

"The shooter must have been on foot," Jack said. "I didn't hear any car sounds before or after the shots."

I shook my head. "Me neither."

"He or she could have parked a street or two away," Jack continued. "Maybe down on Mass. Avenue."

I nodded.

Jack finished his sandwich and pushed his plate to the side. "I also wonder if those shots were intended to frighten, or to warn, instead of to do injury or to kill."

I raised my eyebrows. "Possibly."

"I mean, you can't shoot at a three-story house and expect to zero in on one particular person in it."

"No. Your living-room curtains are opaque. No one could have seen my silhouette through them."

"So the shots are probably in the same category as the doll in your dresser drawer."

"Yes," I said. "A preview of coming attractions."

6

We left the house early the next morning. The unmarked police car took off when we did. Not having had much of a dinner the previous evening, we stopped for a major breakfast at the S and S on Cambridge Street. We each ordered the same thing: two eggs over easy, home fries, rye toast, bacon, and fruit cup. And about a gallon of coffee apiece.

We were in a corner booth behind a service island, far enough from the other patrons so that we didn't have to whisper in order not to be overheard.

"What do you think?" I said.

"About what?"

"Do you think Garrett's the one responsible for the letters and the doll? And for the shooting?"

Jack looked at me over his coffee cup. "He could be. In some ways, he's a much better suspect than anyone else. But— I can also make a very good argument for Wee Willie Walters or somebody connected with his gang. And don't forget Alan Sturgis. Dorothy Evans is a possibility. Wellesley still hasn't given me anything on her, though."

I waved my hand. "Oh, let's write Dorothy off, Jack. I've given some thought to her. I never could see her doing something as gutsy as breaking into my place. And as for shooting at your house—it's hard for me to imagine her doing that, either. I mean, this is a woman whose nickname is Dodo, for God's sake. Okay, all right, when we first got the photo with the scorched eyes, I thought, 'Yeah, this connects with the

Evanses.' But remember I observed Dodo throughout her husband's trial. And my recollection tells me she's a wimp. I mean, she's just not the type to go on a vengeance trip. She'd be more likely to whine to her aerobics instructor."

Jack laughed.

"And as for Alan Sturgis?" I shrugged. "A real dark horse at best. Okay, a week ago he was a possibility. Now—I don't know. I've thought about him, too. He's such a rabbity little pathetic shmuck. Well, rabbity *big* pathetic shmuck."

"They can be the worst," Jack said. "Sturgis had the brains and balls to carry out a major bank fraud."

"Yeah, I know," I said. "The old wolf-in-nerd's-clothing syndrome. But what have we got on him, really, other than the fact that he left the Cape in a big hurry to come back to Boston?"

"That's true."

"Anyway," I said, "the letter writer is someone who's clearly nuts. I told you that Denise Amaral told me that in her opinion Garrett's become increasingly unstable. And Denise should know, Jack. She's worked with him on a daily basis for the past ten years."

Jack nodded.

"So now what do we do?"

Jack smiled. "It's more a matter of what I do."

I nibbled a chunk of cantaloupe from the fruit cup. "What'll that be?"

"I'll call Hibley and ask him to come to my office for a talk."

"Suppose he refuses?"

"Believe me, if he has a choice between him coming to me and me going and getting him—particularly if I decide to go get him while he's at work—he'll come to me."

"Uh-huh. Then what?"

"I'll tell him I have reason to believe he's the author of a series of threatening letters. Then I'll ask him if he has, in fact, written any such letters."

"Suppose he says no?"

"Then I'll tell him that I have a complainant—that's you, cookie—and that we can take the matter to court."

"And?"

"I'll advise him of his rights, tell him I'll see him in court, and release him."

"I see."

"Legally, that's the only course of action open to me."

"Uh-huh."

Jack drank his coffee. "Although there is another track I can take."

"What's that?"

"I can threaten to have him sent for a psychiatric evaluation. We've done that before, in cases like this. You'd be surprised at how effective just the threat of one is."

"At getting guys harassing women to knock it off?"

"Uh-huh. It works maybe nine times out of ten."

I nodded, and looked out the restaurant window across Cambridge Street, at a used-furniture store. "Suppose Garrett proves a tougher nut to crack?" I said to the window.

"Then I go to Plan B."

I looked back at Jack. "What's that?"

"I stomp the shit out of him."

"*All right.*"

We talked a little more, finished our breakfasts, paid the check, and went to the car.

"One thing," Jack said.

"What's that?"

"If you have it in your head to go charging down to Kendall Associates sometime today, gun in purse, looking for Hibley—

forget it. You want to confront him, fine by me. But you'll do it in a courtroom or the C.I.D. All right?"

"Sure. But only if I get to stomp the shit out of him, too."

We drove to the police station. Jack went to the third floor, I headed for the fourth. As I was climbing the stairs, the C.I.D. secretary intercepted me. She held out a folded pink message slip.

I thanked her, taking the paper. Continuing up the stairs, I opened it. The note read: "Please call Laura Deane at the *Globe*." I raised my eyebrows, then shoved the paper into my jacket pocket.

The police academy office was unoccupied. I went to one of the three empty desks and used the phone on it to dial the *Globe* number.

"Hi, what's up?" I said, when Laura came on the line.

"Liz," she said. "Remember the other day when you called to ask me if I'd ever gotten any threatening letters?"

I felt my fingers tighten on the receiver. "And you have since then?"

"No, no, nothing like that. It's just that I was talking to one of the other reporters yesterday, and I was telling him what you told me, and he said that he'd once gotten some threats."

"Oh? With respect to what?"

"A series of articles he'd done on the Jamaican gangs."

I inhaled sharply.

The reporter's name was Harry Cummings. I had never met him, although I had read his stuff. He was an outstanding crime writer.

Laura transferred my call to Cummings's line. As it turned out, *he* was familiar with some of *my* stuff. We exchanged the ritual pleasantries. Then we got down to business.

"I'd like to talk to you more about this," Cummings said. "Is there somewhere we could meet today?"

"Sure," I said. "You name it."

"You're in Cambridge, right?"

"Yes."

"Okay, well, I have to go over there this afternoon. Where will you be?"

"The police station."

He laughed. "Right, where else? Look, I'll come by about three, huh? Meet you at the front desk."

"That's good."

"See you."

I hung up and stared blankly at the wall opposite.

At 2:55, I was leaning on the front desk, chatting idly with a woman officer who'd been a student of mine in the police academy report writing course I'd taught several years ago. At 3:05, a tall skinny guy in chinos and a tweed jacket came through the front doors and up the steps. He had hair just as red as mine, but a lot shorter and a lot curlier.

"Harry," one of the desk officers said. "What's happening?"

This, apparently, was Cummings. I pushed away from the desk and walked toward him. He looked at me and said, "Liz Connors?"

I nodded. "Nice to meet you." We shook hands.

Cummings turned back to the desk to continue speaking to the officer who'd greeted him. I was conscious of an odd feeling of relief—odd because I hadn't realized I'd been nervous or anxious. Had I been worried on some level that Cummings wasn't who he'd claimed to be? Well, he'd just been ID'd by a cop I knew.

Cummings finished his conversation and turned back to me. "You want to talk here or someplace else?"

"I've been cooped up all day," I said. "I'd just as soon get out. What I'd really like to do is walk. Down to the river."

He glanced at his watch. "Yeah, that's okay." He had an abrupt, almost curt way of speaking.

He moved as briskly as he talked. Fortunately I have a long, rapid stride myself.

When we were about a block away from the station, I said, "Tell me about the threats you got."

"They started about two years ago," Cummings replied. "Just after I finished a three-part series on the Boston posses."

"I read it," I said. "It was good."

"Thanks. Anyway, I got the first letter at work. It went—funny how I can remember the exact wording—'you die soon, motherfucker.' "

And soon I'll come to kill you.

"Go on," I said.

"I got one or two letters, a week apart, after that. And a phone call. All saying more or less the same thing."

"I see. Did you save the letters?"

"What, for my scrapbook? No. I gave them to the Boston P.D. and the FBI."

"And? What happened after that?"

"Nothing."

"The letter writer didn't try to follow up on his threat?"

"No. Although I admit I was nervous about starting my car for the next month."

"The posses don't seem to go for ignition bombs," I said. "They prefer guns. Somebody shot at me last night with a nine millimeter."

Cummings gave me a quick, sidelong glance. "That's one of their favorite handguns. The Glock, the Smith and Wesson . . ."

I nodded. "Of course," I said. "Those are the favorite handguns of a lot of non-Jamaican bad guys, too."

We had reached the river, the spot where Memorial Drive and the Western Avenue bridge entrance intersect.

As we crossed the street to the river bank, I said, "I'm pretty sure it isn't somebody from the posses who's after me. But I'm open to the possibility that it might be."

We found an empty bench on the grassy strip beside the river and took it. As we sat down, Cummings said, "Who else do you think might be after you?"

I shrugged, unwilling to be specific with a relative stranger. "I've annoyed a number of people recently." I opened my handbag. "Here. You want to see the letters I've gotten?"

"Sure."

Cummings read through them quickly. When he'd finished, he handed them back to me and said, "Well, the tone is familiar."

"Uh-huh. Harry, did you ever find out who sent you your threats? And made the phone call?"

He shook his head. "No. I have no idea which one of the posses it even was. I mean, Christ, how many of them are here operating in the Boston area now? Ten?"

"Last I counted," I said. "Shower, Dog, Spangler, Jungle, Waterhouse, Kew Gardens, Reema, Spanish Town, Riverton City, and Tel Aviv."

Cummings smiled. "The names are great, aren't they?"

"Divine," I said. "At least we don't have to deal with the Okra Slime."

"The pack that operates out of L.A.?"

"The very one."

Cummings nodded. "Who did you do your article about?"

"Wee Willie Walters and the Dog."

Cummings whistled. "If you've pissed off Wee Willie, you've pissed off a major-leaguer. Worse even than Sugarbaby."

"Who the hell is Sugarbaby?"

"A maniac. He's a big man with the Reema. He killed two cops in New York."

I felt a small chill, thinking of Jack. "Yes, the posses don't have the traditional gang compunctions about killing police, do they?"

"Nope. And they don't seem to have too many compunctions about going after reporters, either." Cummings grimaced. "Makes you nostalgic for the Mafia, doesn't it?"

"Yeah. Harry, why do you suppose whatever posse was after you didn't follow through on its threats?"

"Damned if I know," he said. "Usually they *do* follow through, or try to. Maybe I was lucky. Maybe they decided they had bigger fish to fry. I don't know." He leaned back against the bench, resting his arms along the top. "The threats stopped, though. Maybe they just wanted to scare me."

"Or warn you off doing any future articles on them."

"That too."

I hesitated a moment. "Somebody sent me a photograph of myself with the eyes burned out. And somebody else, maybe the same person, broke into my apartment and left a red-haired doll with a big red x painted on its chest."

"Jesus," Cummings said. "What are you doing to protect yourself?"

"I have a gun. If I have to, I'll use it."

He stared at me. "I hope to hell you're quick on the draw."

"Getting there," I said.

"Good."

Cummings walked with me back to the police station. Outside the front entrance, we shook hands. He told me to take care and keep looking over my shoulder. I said I would. Then he went off to North Cambridge to interview a community group about the rising rate of housebreaks there.

I looked at my watch. It was a little past four. I'd be meeting Jack in his office at five. I figured I'd spend the intervening time over coffee, thinking. I crossed Western Avenue to one of the luncheonettes by the bus stop.

The luncheonette was empty except for two elderly men at a table in the back. I sat down at the counter.

In my purse was a copy of the article I'd written about Walters. I'd intended—but forgotten—to offer it to Cummings.

A photograph of Walters appeared above the article title. It had been taken just after his arrest. Walters had gazed at the photographer with a kind of flat-eyed malevolence. Otherwise there was no expression on his face.

His demeanor had been the same throughout his trial. He had not, of course, taken the stand on his own behalf. He had sat unmoving at the defense table, never even conferring with his lawyer, as still and silent as some massive obsidian carving. His unblinking malignant stare had never wavered from the faces of the prosecution witnesses.

The waitress brought my coffee. Absently, I stirred milk and artificial sweetener into it.

Unlike many of the posse members, Walters wasn't a fugitive from justice in Jamaica. Which was not to say he hadn't committed any crimes there. He probably had.

Also unlike many of the posse members, he had somewhere, somehow, acquired the rudiments of an education. And he was highly intelligent. Eminently capable, as I had noted before, of writing a literate, even slightly poetic death threat. Perhaps it had amused him to do so.

He was reputed to be a model prisoner in Walpole. The guards and all the other inmates were probably scared shitless of him. Even the Cosa Nostra boys doubtless gave him a wide berth.

I flipped through the article, pausing here and there to read a sentence or paragraph. I had devoted a section of the piece to describing the general characteristics of the posses. It was a fairly extensive list: they used aliases and phony places and dates of birth, they gave themselves silly or inapposite nicknames, and they regarded high-powered weapons as status symbols. Although they bought expensive cars and jewelry, they lived quietly in middle-income neighborhoods. The heads and higher-level gang members distanced themselves from the troops—although they commanded the intense loyalty of those troops.

Willie could get any of his guys to do anything for him.

The posses were also clever at adapting to and circumventing the investigating techniques of law-enforcement officials.

It had taken Jack a lot of work and a long time to bring Willie down on that narcotics bust. Actually Jack had been after Willie for one of the four murders he'd committed. The drug arrest was an unexpected byproduct.

I finished my coffee and read the last item: the posses were adept at countersurveillance methods.

I had forgotten that. I put my cup in the saucer and reread the material.

"He could have someone watching you and reporting back to him," Jack had said of Willie.

On the way home from work, Jack and I detoured to my house so I could check the mail and phone messages. The phone messages were all social. The mail was bills and circulars, with one leavening addition—a letter from Matt Aherne, my main source for the exposé I'd written on the Conventicle of Saints.

So swept away had I been by my certainty that it was Garrett after me that I'd shunted Matt and the Conventicle to a corner of my mind. I stared at the envelope for a moment.

"What's up?" Jack said.

"Letter from Matt Aherne."

Jack raised his eyebrows.

"I just spoke to Matt a couple days ago," I said. I looked at the postmark on the envelope. "This was mailed yesterday."

"Maybe he remembered something he forgot to tell you on the phone."

I nodded.

"Or it could be he just wants to ask your advice about some night courses he should take."

"I hope it's that," I said.

It wasn't, quite.

I read the letter over a pre-dinner drink.

It did actually begin with some discussion of whether I thought it would be good for Matt to enroll in Survey of American Lit II next semester or whether Survey of English Lit I might be a better choice.

Following that was news of Theresa and the children, Jason and Tiffany. Theresa had resumed working part-time at her old day-care job in Dartmouth. The twins were apparently in the worst throes of the terrible twos.

At the end of the letter was a brief, almost off-hand mention of something funny that had happened at the auto shop the other day. Matt had gone out to lunch. When he'd returned, one of the other mechanics had given him a message. A man who'd refused to give his name had called the shop and said, simply, "Tell that Aherne fuck he's dead."

I showed the letter to Jack.

"Could be a dissatisfied customer," he said.

"Matt does honest work."

"Sure. I'm not talking about that."

"Right. You mean like somebody who never changes the oil or the antifreeze or who rocks a car with an automatic transmission in the mud or snow and then blames the mechanic because it dies."

Jack smiled. "For someone who doesn't drive, you know a lot about cars. That's right."

I let Matt's letter drop into my lap.

"Probably just a crank call," Jack said.

"Yeah."

The following morning, Denise Amaral called me just as I was getting out of the shower. I went to the phone dabbing and rubbing at myself with a towel and dripping water all over Jack's bedroom floor.

"If you tell me you're up and at 'em already," I said, "I'll puke."

"Open the barf bag," she said. "I signed off on two major research reports before eight-thirty. Liz? I haven't dug up any samples of Garrett's printing yet."

"That's okay," I replied. "If you do, let me know. Jack—my friend in the police department—says he needs to see them."

"I have a few notes from Garrett in script. Would those be useful?"

"They might be." Jack had said something to me about how certain characteristics of an individual's hand could *possibly* remain the same whether he wrote in script or print. He wasn't sure.

"Okay, they're yours," Denise said. "Listen, there's one other thing. This morning I spoke to the woman who was going to file the sexual harassment suit against Garrett. Would you like to talk to her? She's willing."

"I'd *love* to."

"Okay, well, her extension is 235. Give her a call. Her name is Dana Hogan."

"I'll do that. Maybe she can meet me for lunch today. Thanks."

"Good luck."

*   *   *

The delicatessen in the basement of the American Twine Company building was, at one o'clock, medium-crowded. Even so, I had no trouble picking Dana Hogan out of the throng. She had described herself well.

She was very small—no more than five-one—thin, and sparrow-boned. Her hair was fine and light brown, in a shoulder-length Dutch-boy cut. Her pale face was heart-shaped, with full pink lips and silky dark brows arched in permanent surprise over large blue eyes. She wore jeans and a loden-length parka with sheepskin collar and cuffs. She looked about eighteen, but I knew that as a senior research associate at Bioline she had to be at least twenty-seven or twenty-eight.

She shook my hand. Her fingers were chilly and twiglike.

Most of the deli patrons were getting their food to go, so we had no problem getting a table.

I ordered a spinach salad. Dana Hogan had hummus and tabouli with pita bread.

"Want to eat first and talk later?" I asked. "Or eat and talk simultaneously?"

Dana Hogan smiled. "Eat and talk is fine. I have to get back to the lab by two at the latest."

"Okay. Now, did Denise tell you anything about my situation?"

Hogan nodded slowly, her eyes searching my face.

"What happened with you?" I asked. "When did it begin?"

She ate some hummus on a triangle of bread before replying. "About a year ago."

"I see."

"I was assigned to the project team Garrett was heading up. Me and four others. I was the only female in the group. We were working on developing an alternative vaccine for—well, I shouldn't be too specific about what we were doing."

"You don't have to be. It doesn't matter, for my purposes."

She nodded. "Anyway, I'd been on the team for about a month, and one night I stayed late to run some tests, and Garrett was there, too, working on some things, and around eight or nine we both called it quits. He asked me if I wanted to go someplace for dinner with him. So we did, and afterward we went for a drink, and it was a nice time." She looked at me. "Garrett can be very charming, you know?"

"Yeah. I know."

"Well, so after that, we started going out together, a few times a week. It was no heavy relationship, but it was fun. I guess we dated for about a month."

"And then?"

She picked at the tabouli with a plastic fork. "I think I was a little uncomfortable about getting involved with a guy who was technically my boss. Also, I'd just recently broken up with a man I'd lived with for three years, and I wasn't really ready for another big affair."

I nodded.

"So I ended it with Garrett. I tried to be nice about it. I explained to him about my ex-boyfriend and all."

"Was he upset? Angry?"

Hogan shook her head. "No, not at all." She smiled wryly. "He was very civilized."

I nodded again.

"About a week after that, all the shit started to happen at work."

"Like what?"

"Oh, minor at first. Garrett was kind of cool to me. But I figured that was understandable, given the circumstances."

"Sure."

"Then . . . he started shutting me out."

I frowned. "Of what?"

Hogan chewed a pita crust, reflectively. "Our project group

meetings. It was very subtle at first. I'd say something and he'd ignore it. Then that sort of escalated to where every time I opened my mouth, he'd roll his eyes or shake his head and, you know, look exasperated. Like he was asking himself why did he have to waste his time listening to this silly broad?"

"Uh-huh."

"Then he started to criticize my work. Tell me I wasn't running a sequence of tests properly, or that I was running them too quickly, or too slowly."

"Yes?"

"The thing was, he'd yell at me in front of the others. It was as if he was deliberately trying to humiliate me. Anyone else whose work wasn't up to par, he always talked to *them* about it in private."

"I see."

Hogan took a deep breath. "I knew I wasn't screwing up my work."

"What about the other guys on the project team? What did they think?"

Hogan shrugged and looked scornful. "Oh, they saw what was going on. But none of them were going to challenge Garrett. Oh no."

"Right."

"Then one day I came to work and found that one of my experiments had been tampered with."

"Good God."

"Yeah. It's too complicated to explain, but basically, what happened is that a compound I was testing got adulterated. Which of course invalidated the whole experiment. I'd just spent about two months on it."

I shook my head slowly.

"Well, of course I couldn't prove that it had been sabotaged," Hogan continued, her voice flat and dry. "The tampering had been done in such a way as to look like the result of carelessness on my part." She inhaled sharply again. "I could have been fired right then and there."

"What happened?"

"Denise went to bat for me. She knew what was going on. Neither of us could prove that Garrett had been the one who messed up the experiment, though."

"No."

"Then I started getting phone calls late at night."

"Obscene? Threatening?"

"No, nothing like that. In fact, nothing at all, except somebody breathing on the other end of the line."

"Did the calls follow a regular pattern?"

"No. Sometimes there'd be one or two in a single night, and then he'd skip a day, and there'd be another, then skip two days, and there'd be three. Like that."

"Did you tell the phone company?"

She shook her head. "I was going to, but the calls stopped. This only went on for a little over a week."

"And you think Garrett was the caller?"

"Oh, sure. I just couldn't *prove* it."

"Okay. What about work?"

"Things between Garrett and me got worse. He was on my case constantly. It got so bad that one of the guys on the project team even finally said something to Garrett. Garrett told him to mind his own business, or words to that effect."

"What about anybody else in the company, other than Denise?"

Hogan laughed slightly. "Garrett was their superstar. I was just a research associate. And pretty new to the place."

"Sure. Were you ever tempted to quit?"

"Dozens of times. But"—she toyed with the remains of the food on her plate—"I knew that was exactly what *he* wanted me to do."

"Of course. So you hung in there. Good for you."

"Denise got me transferred to another project. And she said she'd support me if I charged harassment."

I sighed. "That must have been painful for her, too. She and Garrett were buddies for a long time."

Hogan nodded. "I know. I felt rotten about putting her in the middle."

"Well, you didn't have much choice. And obviously, she felt you were in the right."

"Yes."

We were quiet for a few moments, I sipping my coffee and Hogan her tea.

"The thing is," Hogan said.

"Yes? What?"

She put down her cup. "I'll always wonder *why*. Why he did that to me."

"I can tell you that."

She looked at me.

"You rejected him," I said. "Superstars don't like being rejected."

"But I—"

"I know, I know. You're looking at it from your point of view and not from the point of view of someone with an ego the size of the Rock of Gibralter. You rejected Garrett. And for that you had to pay."

"Is that what happened with you and him?"

I smiled. "No. The other way around. He rejected me. And he didn't try to be civilized about it, either. In fact, he tried to be as cruel as possible. Which he turned out to be expert at."

"I'm sorry."

I shrugged. "You got punished for one thing, I for another."

That huge ego hadn't come from nowhere. He had always been Golden Boy.

His brilliance, like his physical beauty and strength, had been manifest early. And as if those natural gifts hadn't been enough, he had come from a rich and fairly prominent New York family. The prep school he'd attended had educated his father and grandfather. In his four years there, he had garnered more scholarly and athletic trophies than his two predecessors combined. College was a glorified extension of the same.

He had never boasted of any of this. I'd only found out about it gradually, as we'd begun to exchange the stories of our lives. In bits and pieces, naturally, as the subject arose.

My background wasn't nearly as flossy as his. Close enough, though, for us to understand each other's points of reference.

Like me, he was the eldest of four children. But perhaps that was where our most basic differences began.

He'd once joked to me that growing up with three worshipful younger sisters and an equally devoted mother had been like being a sultan in possession of a small and ultra-exclusive harem.

Throwaway line though it had been, the remark stayed with me.

He never mentioned the subject, but I could only imagine that he must have been one of Manhattan's more highly sought-after escorts to all the coming-out parties.

And I had seen, vividly, the way women looked at him when he and I went to public places together.

Every woman, central to or on the fringes of his life, had adored him unquestioningly.

Until me.

And far worse than my failure to adore him blindly was the fact that I had written for all the world to read that the gold was only plate over base metal.

7

A memory.

It was the first time Garrett and I had slept together. Afterward, we lay in bed, murmuring the little languid dopey things to each other that lovers do in those circumstances. Suddenly Garrett had shoved himself up on one elbow and stared down at me. Then he started to snicker.

"What's so funny?" I'd asked.

He shook his head. "I'm laughing because your eyes are the exact same color as mine."

I never could figure out why I found that remark so absolutely endearing.

When I got back to the police station, I poked my head into Jack's office.

He said, "I called Hibley at Kendall Associates, first thing I got in today."

"And?"

"He's not there."

"What?"

Jack smiled. "No, he hasn't quit them. Or disappeared. He's out of town on a business trip. He'll be away for the rest of the week."

"Where'd he go?"

"Chicago."

"When'd he leave?"

"This morning."

*   *   *

I went upstairs, and for the next two hours thought long and hard about what Dana Hogan had told me.

It was four o'clock, and I was back in Jack's office, taking a late coffee break with him, when the phone rang. He picked up the receiver and said, "Lieutenant Lingemann." He listened for a moment to whoever was on the other end of the line, grinned, and said, "Same to you, gorgeous. What can I do for you?"

The caller replied at some length. Jack listened. And as he listened, his smile faded.

The call, though it had started out on a humorous note, had apparently turned into a business one. I jerked my head at the office door and hissed, "Would you like me to leave so you can talk in private?"

He shook his head violently. I settled back in my chair and stared at him. And noted how the lines on his long, hard-boned face seemed to deepen.

"Yeah," he said into the phone. "I know. Look, I'll talk to you later. Right. Uh-huh. For Christ's sake, *be careful*. Yeah. 'Bye."

He hung up the receiver and looked at me.

"What was that all about?" I said.

He took a deep breath. "That was Cassie."

"Cassie Stewart? The ADA?"

He nodded.

"What's wrong?" I said.

"She got another threat on her life today."

"Oh, God."

"Somebody called her at work. She was in court, so they left a message with the switchboard operator."

"What was it?"

" 'Bitch, we're going to kill you real soon.' "

*   *   *

I spent the remainder of the afternoon in my cubbyhole on the fourth floor.

Not writing.

Thinking some more.

"What are you going to do about Cassie?" I asked Jack, as we walked to his car.

He shrugged. "You know Cass. She's tough. She doesn't want protection any more than you did."

"She may need it as much as you think I do."

"I know." Jack unlocked the passenger door of the car. "That's why I asked a couple of the guys who patrol near where she lives to keep an eye on her. Unobtrusively."

"Good."

We drove out onto Western Avenue. The rush-hour traffic in Central Square was, as always, appalling.

"Do we need to stop at the grocery store for anything?" Jack asked.

"Don't think so. The dinner we didn't have the other night is still waiting to be made."

"Okay."

I was silent while he negotiated the car through the gridlock.

"Jack?"

"Yes?"

"I don't think the threats on Cassie's life are related to the ones on mine."

He glanced at me. "Coincidence that you're both getting them?"

"Yes. All right, I agree, Wee Willie Walters *is* a link between Cass and me. And, yes, he *is* vicious and vengeful. But . . . Cass has put a lot of bad guys away. And some of them have been real maniacs too. It could be one of them out to get her.

Or maybe some guy she's currently prosecuting. Or one of his relatives or buddies."

"Maybe."

"Even if it is Walters who's threatening to kill her—that doesn't necessarily mean he's threatening to kill me, too."

"Don't be too sure. There's a lot of similarity between the wording of the threats against Cassie and the ones against you. In her case, 'Bitch, we're going to kill you real soon,' and in your case, 'And soon I'll come to kill you.' That's close, babe. Very close."

"Yeah, I know, I know. Look, I just have this absolute dead certainty that in my case, it's Garrett. Let me tell you what I learned about him from the woman I had lunch with today."

"Go ahead."

I did.

When we got to Jack's place, he took Lucy out to the back yard to run around and relieve herself. I took a container of veal and chicken chunks, onions, mushrooms, and chicken broth out of the refrigerator and put the contents in a pot to heat slowly. Then I made drinks, and set out a bowl of food for the dog.

Jack and I took our drinks to the living room. Neither of us was the type to burrow in a closet or the cellar just because shots had been fired at the house last night. We lived the way we lived, and that was that.

Still, before we sat down, I checked the gun in my purse. I was doing that more and more frequently, lately.

Good to know it was there.

The shattered window panes had been replaced by the landlord. I pulled the draperies. Jack built a fire, and we sat down on the hearth rug before it.

"By the way," Jack said. "I checked. Hibley doesn't have a gun permit or an F.I.D. card."

I sipped my drink. "I'm not surprised. He would hardly have used a gun registered in his own name to shoot at us. Sort of a dead giveaway, that."

"No fooling?"

"It's him, Jack. I know it's him."

He nodded.

"Do you want to hear another reason why I think that?"

"Sure."

"Remember when I got the photo of me with the eyes burned out?"

He grimaced. "It's not something I'm likely to forget."

I looked down at my glass. "There was something Garrett used to say to me all the time."

"What was that?"

"He was always telling me how beautiful he thought my eyes were."

Another memory:

A few months after I'd met him, Garrett had asked me for a picture of myself. I'd rummaged around until I'd found a halfway decent black-and-white snapshot that didn't make me look like something hanging off a cornice of Notre Dame cathedral. I offered that to him.

He shook his head. "Nope. No good. Take it back."

"What's wrong with it?"

"I can't look at it and see the color of your hair."

"You're awfully quiet," Jack said. "What's on your mind?"

I gave myself a little shake. "Nothing. Fleeting thought."

Jack called Garrett's home number. On the fifth ring, an answering machine responded. I was listening in on the bedroom extension. The sound of Garrett's mechanically reproduced voice gave me an almost electric shock.

Jack left no message.
Neither did I.

I stirred sour cream, powdered garlic, and Hungarian pa-
prika into the veal and chicken mixture. While that heated
through, I boiled some noodles. Jack set the table.

"Say it is Hibley who's doing this to you," Jack said. "What
do you think is going on in his head?"

"I was hoping you could help me with that."

"*Me? I'm* not crazy, babe."

"No. But you're a man, and so is Garrett."

Jack looked at me thoughtfully. "Okay. I see what you
mean."

I swished a wooden spoon through the noodles. "Last night,
when I was telling you about how Garrett and I broke up, I
told you the occasion was a dinner to celebrate me getting my
first two articles published."

"A dinner *you* cooked," Jack said. "Couldn't he have taken
you out, or something?"

I shrugged. "Well, that's beside the point. Anyhow, when
I was telling you this, I got the distinct impression from you
that you thought Garrett wasn't happy about my articles, despite what he said to the contrary."

"He was needling you about being a literary star, wasn't
he?"

"Uh-huh."

"Well," Jack said, "that indicates to me that Hibley was
pretty damn displeased with your success, then."

"But why wouldn't he have been? Pleased, I mean."

Jack glanced at me. "Competitiveness."

"Oh, Jack. Why would he feel that way? I wasn't competing
with him. He was—is—a scientist, for Christ's sake. I'm a
writer. Formerly an English professor."

"Doesn't matter what your field is," Jack said. "There are

men who hate women who succeed at anything except maybe cooking and having babies."

"They see any professional success—even one not in their own area—as competition?"

"Right."

I pursed my lips, sourly. "I know that, I guess. I just have trouble believing it. It seems so idiotic. Not to say irrational. Garrett always prided himself on his rationality."

Jack laughed. "A lot of cuckoo clocks do."

I served the food and we sat down at the table.

"That means," I said, "that Garrett found me lovable when I was a failure—although failure's too strong a word . . ."

"I understand what you mean."

"But repellent when I was a success. Or at least on the verge of becoming a success."

"Yup."

"Swell. So why, then, did he tell me that the reason he didn't want to be with me anymore was that he loved me?"

"I admit," Jack said, "when you told me that, it threw me a little, too. But I've had a chance to think about it, and maybe it had something to do with him being genuinely scared of a feeling he couldn't control."

I sighed. "Garrett did like to control things."

"I'm sure he did. You being one of the things."

I smiled at Jack. "So how come *you* never try to control me?"

He looked at me quite seriously. "Because if I did, you'd take a hike."

We took coffee into the living room. Jack added a log to the fire. Lucy parked on the hearth rug, so we took the two wing chairs.

"You know," I said, "the connecting thread here is Garrett's egomania. It made him reject me, and attack Dana Hogan for rejecting him. And now he's after me again, because I wrote about him and, in his eyes, held him up to public scrutiny in a *very* unflattering light."

"If he's writing you threatening letters and putting dead dolls in your underwear drawer and shooting at you, then he's not just an egomaniac," Jack said. "He's fucking crazy."

"That's what I've been saying all along."

We drank our coffee.

Yet another memory:

Garrett and I had had dinner in a Harvard Square restaurant. It was the first really warm spring evening, so, after we finished eating, we decided to go for a walk.

The square was like a giant open-air party. Or maybe an open-air circus. There was a strong smell of popcorn. The street musicians were offering something for everyone: jazz, folk, rock, chamber. There was a player piano in the middle of the Brattle Square island jangling out ragtime. There was, literally, dancing in the streets. The warm breeze had fanned a fever in blood chilled too long by the winter.

Garrett and I, smiling like everyone else, threaded our way through the crowd, past Out of Town News and the subway station, and down Holyoke Street. We crossed Mount Auburn and went into a small, narrow, alley-like street.

"Where are we going?" I said.

"For an after-dinner drink," Garrett said.

I looked around us. On all sides were Harvard buildings. "Where? In a dorm room?"

"You'll see."

We crossed a large green space to another brick building. The sign over the door read ELIOT HOUSE.

"What is this?" I said, laughing.

"The one bar in Cambridge you've never been to," Garrett said. "Follow me."

I did, down a short corridor. He pulled a ring of keys from his pocket, selected one, and unlocked a door. He opened it, put a hand lightly between my shoulder blades, and ushered me into a high-ceilinged, wood-paneled room with a fireplace, leather chairs and couch, and long windows that looked out on Memorial Drive and the Charles.

"My God," I said. "From what English murder mystery did they steal *this* setup?"

Garrett laughed. "Sit down. What would you like?"

"What are you offering?"

He shrugged. "Whatever you like."

I deliberated. "Well, it's not something I usually drink. But given the environment, anything else would be a desecration. Bristol Cream. But make it a double, on the rocks. With a chunk of lime, if it's available."

He left the room, going down another hall that led off to the right. I sat down on the couch facing the fireplace. The leather was a bit slippery. There was a brass ship's clock on the wall to the right of the mantel. It didn't give the correct time.

Garrett reappeared with two glasses. "No lime," he said, handing me my glass.

"I'll cope," I said.

He had what looked like scotch on the rocks, his customary drink. He sat down next to me.

"What is this place?" I asked.

"Senior Common Room of Eliot House."

"Oh. And it has a bar?"

He nodded to the right. "There's a little kitchen in there. That's where the drink stuff is."

"I see. So why do you have a key to it?"

"I'm an affiliate of the House," he explained. "I was a tutor in chemistry here when I was a graduate student. I lived here as an undergraduate."

"Oh, really? I thought Eliot was the literary house."

"Well, they let the odd science major in. Occasionally. For variety."

"For the variety you offer, I can't speak," I said. "You sure as hell are odd, though. They got their money's worth on that part of the deal."

He grinned, shaking his head. He liked it when I teased him.

"Seriously," I said, "what does being an affiliate of the House entail?"

He shrugged. "Nothing, really. It's honorary. I can show up for dinner here on Tuesday nights and lunch on Fridays."

"Do you?"

"Hardly ever. I don't have the time."

I leaned back against the cool, slick surface of the couch. "Well, it's a lovely room. I wouldn't mind hanging out here. My compliments to Dr. Eliot and his five-foot shelf." I held up my glass. "This is nice, but it isn't Bristol Cream."

"Savory and James."

"As I said before, I'll cope."

He put his arm around me. I rested my head against his shoulder.

"I got some news today," Garrett said.

I moved my head to the right to look at him. "Oh, really? What's that?"

"You remember I told you about that big contract we were trying to land with the Genetics Research Institute?"

"Of course." I raised my head. "What about it?"

He took his arm from behind my neck, rose, and stood in front of me. He moved, as always, with a kind of long, lean, languid grace. His curly, blond-streaked brown hair shone in the muted lamplight. His slightly slanted green eyes glittered. Perhaps with excitement. Maybe triumph.

He made a thumbs-up gesture at me with the hand that wasn't holding his drink.

I took a deep breath. "You got it," I said. "You got the contract. My God. Oh, Garrett, that's wonderful. That's great." I put my glass on the end table, jumped up, and hugged him. He grabbed me very tightly. I leaned against him. He put his head back and laughed. It was a sound of pure exultation.

"Why didn't you tell me before?" I asked.

"I was saving it for the right moment."

"And this is it?"

"We're alone."

"Yes," I said. "We are." I reared back slightly and looked at him. "Garrett, this is just marvelous." I put my right hand up to his face. "It's wonderful. My God. What this will mean to cancer research."

"Mmmm," he said, smiling down at me.

"And it's all your doing. If it weren't for you . . . *you're* wonderful. Oh, God. I know how hard you had to work for this. My God, this will be some of the most important medical research in . . . in human history. And it'll be you at the head of it."

He pulled me in against him and kissed me. The kiss had a kind of deep, voracious hunger to it. As we stood pressed together, I could feel his erection.

"You're in a mood to celebrate," I murmured, my mouth against his.

"I am."

"How about here and now?"

He took a deep breath and stared at me. "Are you serious?"

"Absolutely." I moved against him.

"You're beautiful," he said. "I love you."

"He hates me," I said. "Believe it, Jack."

*   *   *

The final memory:

Garrett spun out of bed and began to dress, in very quick, jerky movements. I lay back quivering, feeling pummeled.

"Garrett . . ."

"Shut up. Just shut the fuck up." He was buttoning his shirt.

I got out of bed, yanking the top sheet free of the mattress and wrapping it around me. This was not a time to be naked and vulnerable.

"Garrett, you can't leave like this."

He tucked the shirt into his jeans. "I will do whatever I fucking well want to." He looked at me. "What the hell are you posing in that sheet for, a sculpture? You think your ass is that great?"

I could feel myself shrink, my insides disintegrating.

"Oh, for Christ's sake," he said. "Stop looking so pathetic. You're turning my stomach."

Pride, anger, or a combination of the two flared up through the suffocating hurt. "Goddamn you, two hours ago you told me you loved me."

"Yeah, well, I lied, okay? You want to know what you are to me? What you were to me? A nice, convenient, easy lay. That's all. And now I've had enough of you. I want something else. What I got from you, I can pick up anytime, anywhere. Got that? Is that understood?"

"I know you don't like talking about it," Jack said, "but you're going to have to tell me more about the night you broke up with Hibley."

"You've already heard most of it."

"Yes, well, tell me what I haven't heard. Liz, this is im-protant. If Hibley really is the one after you, I have to know as much as possible about him."

"Yeah, all right."

"Now, you told me he was 'wild' that night. That he didn't

even look like himself. That he ripped you apart. Take it from there."

How was it he'd looked?

It was the eyes, mostly. The green of them was as primitive as sea water. And in the depths, ugly creatures swam. Things long hidden from the light, roiling now to the surface.

I didn't move toward him, but he put his hands up, as if to ward me off, or push me back if I tried to approach.

I was in such pain that I could barely breathe. But I could still think. And on some level, I knew that what I was hearing was coming from a realm outside pure sanity.

That knowledge did not lessen the pain. It gave dimension to the fear beginning to throb beneath it, a fear that if I spoke, or even stirred, the room would explode in a flash of blue-white violence.

His pleasure in reviling me was almost sensual. Sexual? A substitute for what had failed to happen in the bed?

His voice was a purulent discharge.

"You're not fucking getting the message, are you? You make me ill. Everything about you revolts me. I hate the way you look, I hate the way you talk, I hate the way you act. You're a worthless, stupid twat. Like that garbage you write."

He lowered his hands. "Don't ever come near me again. I don't want to catch a glimpse of your face even in a crowd. If you see me, you turn and walk in the opposite direction. No. You run."

"And then he left?" Jack said.

I nodded.

Jack took his arm from my shoulders and patted me lightly on the thigh. "Sorry you had to go through all that." He smiled faintly. "I mean, experiencing it as well as telling it."

I shrugged. "Did you learn anything?"

"Well, you were right in thinking there was something seriously wrong with him, back then. That kind of behavior is beyond abnormal. At least, from my perspective, it is."

"Whatever was wrong with him, it's apparently only gotten worse with the passage of time. He'll be back from Chicago in a few days. What are we going to do?"

"I can still call him into the office and ask him about the letters."

"And the doll? And the photograph?"

"Those too."

"He'll deny it all, you know. Very plausibly."

"Sure. But, as I said before, the fact that he knows we're onto him may throw a scare into him."

"But we can't *prove* he did anything. And, given the fact that he's crazy, how easy will he be to scare?"

Denise Amaral had sent, by courier, her samples of Garrett's handwriting to the police station. These went to the crime lab. We were still waiting for word back from the graphologist. If he could confirm that the handwriting on the memos and the printing on the letters were by the same person, we had a piece of evidence.

8

At eight o'clock that night I got a hysterical phone call from Theresa Aherne. Between sobs she told me that Matt had been killed three hours earlier in a car crash on Route 89 just outside of West Lebanon, New Hampshire.

I was distraught.

Jack tried to calm me down. "Liz, it was an accident."

"But Matt was a good driver."

"He could still have had an accident."

"Right after he was threatened? Isn't that a little coincidental?"

"There's no evidence the one had anything to do with the other."

I shook my head. "I bet the damn Conventiclers sabotaged his car."

"Liz, it was raining. His left rear tire blew out. He skidded on the wet pavement and hit a guardrail."

"Blowouts can be rigged."

Jack sighed. "Look, I know how you feel. It's awful. But it's *not your fault*."

"I keep thinking it is."

"That's ridiculous. Even if—what the hell's his name again? The Conventicle leader?"

"Ray Bamford."

"Yeah, Bamford. Look, even if Bamford had personally gone after Matt and killed him, it *still* wouldn't be your fault. Remember Matt came to you. Remember he told you you could quote him and use his name. Remember he wanted you to write about him."

"Yeah." I got up and went to the bathroom to throw some cold water on my face. When I returned to the living room, Jack gave me a curious look.

"Are you starting to think it's the Conventicle that's after you, now? And not Hibley?"

I shook my head. "No. Not really. But that doesn't mean that Ray and Ella Mae wouldn't want to avenge themselves against Matt. What he said about them was pretty lurid. And he was a convenient target for them. More so than I am."

Jack smiled wryly. "You mean you don't believe they'd show him Christian forgiveness?"

"Bullshit."

I went back up to my cubbyhole to write. I wasn't at my most productive, but it was better than biting my nails. And brooding about Matt. Anyhow, I was on deadline.

Nice phrase.

"Are you really sure you want to be here?" Jack said.

"Positive," I said. I sat, very erect, in the chair by the filing cabinet in Jack's office. My hands were folded in my lap.

I was wearing the slickest outfit I owned, an Italian black wool jersey dress. This was an occasion for which I wanted to look very, very good.

Vanity's a funny thing.

"Your face is a little pale," Jack added.

"It's a reflection of the way I feel. Don't worry. I won't faint or throw a fit."

"All right. Listen—let me do the talking, at least to begin with."

The desk phone rang. Jack picked up the receiver and said, "Lieutenant Lingemann." He listened a moment. "Okay,

Charlene, send him in." He replaced the receiver and looked at me. "Ready?"

I nodded.

There was a knock on the door.

"Come in," Jack said.

The door opened and Garrett stepped into the room. He looked at Jack. Then he looked at me.

"Dr. Hibley," Jack said. "Thanks for dropping by. Have a seat, please." He indicated the chair in front of his desk.

Garrett was still looking at me. His face was blankly unreadable.

"Hello, Liz," he said. His voice wasn't cool. It was neutral.

I nodded again, stiffly.

In seven years, Garrett had gained perhaps ten pounds, a few faint lines on his face, and lost none of his attractiveness. The almond-shaped green eyes were still brilliant, the blond-brown hair still thick and curly. The only real difference was that he was dressed more as a businessman now than as a research scientist, in a gray suit. He had a trenchcoat folded over his left arm.

"Dr. Hibley," Jack said easily. "If we could get started?"

"Of course," Garrett said. "I'm eager to get all this cleared up." He sat down in the chair in front of Jack's desk. His way of moving had not lost its easeful grace.

"All right, now," Jack said. "Dr. Connors has received a series of obscene and threatening letters over the past few weeks. Are you responsible for writing and sending them to her?"

Garrett whipped his head around to stare at me. "What?" The blankness was gone from his face now, replaced by something approaching or approximating shocked perplexity.

Jack repeated himself.

"My God," Garrett said. He faced Jack. "Is this a joke?"

Jack shook his head.

"Of course not. Why would I do such a thing?"

"I was hoping you could tell us that," Jack replied.

"How could I? I have no idea what you're talking about."

"Someone also sent Dr. Connors a photo of her with the eyes burned out," Jack said. "Was that you?"

Garrett moved his head from side to side very slowly, as if disbelieving what he was hearing.

"Someone also broke into Dr. Connors's apartment and left a red-haired doll, apparently intended to represent Dr. Connors herself, in a dresser drawer. The doll had a red cross painted on its chest. Do you know anything about that?"

"This is ridiculous," Garrett said. He turned to stare at me again.

"Dr. Hibley," Jack said mildly, "I should tell you that we can take this matter to court if it's not settled here."

"There's nothing to settle," Garrett said. "I haven't seen or spoken to this woman in years. Much less would I write any kind of a letter to her. This is absurd. I assume you have what you think is proof of these allegations?"

Jack looked at him.

"I'd like to see the letters," Garrett said.

Jack continued to look at him.

The room was very quiet for a few seconds. Garrett flicked a brief glance at me. "If you're not going to show me the letters," he said to Jack, "how do I know they even exist?"

"They're in the state police crime lab," Jack said. "Being analyzed."

Garrett nodded. "Well, that's convenient. And *this* is a waste of my time." He started to rise.

"Sit down, Dr. Hibley," Jack said calmly. His eyes and Garrett's locked. For just a moment, Garrett remained in his semi-elevated pose, like a freeze-frame of an action shot. Then he lowered himself back down onto the chair.

Jack said, "You deny having written and sent the letters?"

Garrett made an exasperated noise. "Of course I deny it."

"And you *didn't* enter Dr. Connors's apartment and leave a doll there?"

"Of course I didn't."

"And you *didn't* send Dr. Connors a photograph of her with the eyes burned out?"

"No, I did not," Garrett said.

Jack nodded. "Okay." He folded his arms and leaned back in his chair.

Garrett gave me another glance and then looked back at Jack. "Tell me, Lieutenant," he said, "is it the practice of this police department to subject innocent people to interrogation on a whim?"

Jack frowned, as if he were giving the question real consideration. He tugged his lower lip between thumb and forefinger. "Nope," he said, finally. "I can't recall ever having seen anything in the General Orders to that effect."

Garrett's eyes narrowed. "You've dragged me in here and made not only ludicrous but completely unsubstantiated charges against me. I call that whimsical. I call it harassment."

"Dr. Connors has reason to believe you've been harassing *her*."

"She may also believe the earth is flat," Garrett said. "Her beliefs have nothing to do with me. They're her problem."

Jack sighed. "Dr. Hibley, I don't think you fully understand. This is serious business. I can have you sent for a psychiatric evaluation."

Garrett's face reddened slightly, just above the cheekbones. "*You* are telling *me* that you can have *me* ordered to undergo observation simply because"—he jerked his head at me—"this woman has suddenly, God knows why, decided to accuse me of sending her obscene mail?"

" 'Fraid so," Jack said.

"My God," Garrett said. "I'm living in a police state. Lieutenant, *I* have rights."

"Thanks for reminding me," Jack said. "I was just about to read them to you."

When he'd finished, Garrett said coldly, "Now what? Am I under arrest?"

"No," Jack said. "You can go."

Garrett stood up, abruptly and angrily.

"Thanks for coming by," Jack said.

Garrett moved toward the door. He paused there, his hand hovering by the knob. "I'll be seeing a lawyer about this."

"Good idea," Jack replied. "You're going to need one."

"I told you he'd lie like a bastard," I said.

Jack nodded. "Don't they all."

"He also knows damn well we don't have anything on him. So what did we accomplish?"

"We taught him something he *didn't* know," Jack said. "That being that we're on to him."

Later that afternoon, the state police graphologist called Jack. The result of the analysis he'd run on Garrett's script and the printing of the letters was . . . inconclusive. He was, he said, sorry not to be able to come up with a firm "yes" or a firm "no," but that there were far too many variables on either side. What he really needed was another print sample. He suggested we get a second opinion from a private specialist.

So it was my word against Garrett's.

I could just imagine me being questioned in court by Garrett's attorney.

"Dr. Connors, refresh my memory. You once had a personal relationship with Dr. Hibley, is that correct?"

"Yes."

"And that relationship was terminated by Dr. Hibley, is that also correct?"

"Yes, he—"

"Just answer the question, *yes* or *no*."

"Yes."

"I see. Now, is it also true that you yourself wanted the relationship with Dr. Hibley to continue?"

"I didn't see any reason for it to end the way it did."

"But you *did* want the relationship to continue."

and:

"Dr. Connors, let's return to the night your relationship with Dr. Hibley ended. You were highly upset, in hysterical condition. You begged him to reconsider."

"I—"

"Yes or no, Dr. Connors."

"I didn't beg—"

or:

"Dr. Connors, how old were you at the time your relationship with Dr. Hibley ended?"

"Thirty."

"Ah. Thirty. Now, could you refresh my memory and that of the court and tell us again your present age?"

"Thirty-seven."

"Have you ever been married?"

"Objection!"

"Objection sustained."

"Dr. Connors, do you have children?"

"Objection!"

"Objection sustained."

"Your Honor, I am merely trying to establish facts about the plaintiff's life and past that might reveal her motives for . . ."

With infinite care, the lawyer would paint me into a corner, limning me as a lovesick lonely neurotic whose biological clock was ticking louder and louder. And at the last he would hold up before the jury a portrait of a woman driven by obsession to avenge herself against the man who'd rejected her.

I thought it would be preferable to go on receiving hate mail and worse than hate mail, and take my chances with what happened thereafter.

"Wait a minute," I said. "How come you didn't ask Garrett if he was the one who shot at your house?"

Jack smiled. "It's always good to hold one thing back. Throws them off balance."

On the way home, he said, "I almost forgot. I got a call this morning from Teddy Byrne."

"Teddy . . . ?" I frowned. "Oh, sure. Teddy Byrne. The guy on the Arlington Police force. What'd he want?"

"Just to tell me he's been keeping an eye on Alan Sturgis."

Despite the way I was feeling, I had to smile. "So what's old Supernerd the Computer Jockey been up to?"

"Harassing a woman."

"*What?*"

Jack stopped for a light at the intersection of Hampshire and Prospect. He put his right hand up to his ear. "If you promise not to screech like that again, I'll tell you."

"Absolutely."

"All right," Jack said. "Well, you know Sturgis has been staying with his parents for the past few weeks because of his mother's heart operation and all."

"Mm-hmm."

"He's been spending his evenings in the town library."

"Doing what, pillaging the computer magazine collection?"

"Jerking off over the centerfold in *PC World*, for all I know," Jack replied. "Anyway, all jokes aside, he got into a conversation with the reference librarian one night. Asked her for help finding a book or something."

"Uh-huh."

"And, well, after that he'd try to strike up a chat with her every time he came into the library. At first she thought he was just a harmless eccentric. Then one night he asked her to go for coffee after the library closed. And she said she couldn't. So he asked her if she'd like to go to a movie some time. And she said she couldn't. So he invited her to dinner."

"And she said she couldn't," I finished. "Sturgis doesn't take hints very well, does he?"

"Then," Jack continued, "he started doing things like waiting outside the library for her, and following her to her car. And writing her notes."

I was silent for a moment. "Notes?" I said, finally.

"Yeah. Things that said, 'I really like you. Can't we go out some time?' Or, 'I know a restaurant that you'd like. Let me take you there.' "

"What happened then?"

"The librarian told Sturgis to cut the shit and leave her alone. She finally blew up at him when she found him hanging around her car one night for about the fourteenth time."

"I see."

"So he stopped following her, and he stopped asking her out. But she's still getting these little notes."

"From Sturgis?"

Jack glanced at me. "I'd guess so. The thing is, they aren't signed."

9

The funeral of Matt Aherne was held in Claremont, New Hampshire, at the oldest Roman Catholic church in the state. Jack and I attended.

The day was sunny and unseasonably warm for early November, which pleased me even in my sadness. The officiating priest was young and fresh-faced, which pleased me too. It seemed appropriate.

There was a good crowd in the church. A mixture of young, middle-aged, and elderly. I wondered if any of them were former Conventiclers.

Theresa Aherne sat with Matt's parents. She looked wretched. The senior Ahernes looked . . . bewildered. As if they'd stumbled into somebody else's nightmare.

One of the altar boys wore red-and-white Nikes beneath his cassock.

"When Matthew was baptized, he put on Christ . . ."

During Communion, Jack and I and the other non-Catholics remained seated. Jack put his arm around me. I looked at the coffin.

Take care of yourself, Matt. Keep an eye out.

Theresa left the church between her mother-in-law and father-in-law. She saw me as she was about to step into the limousine. Our gazes locked for several seconds. Then she came over to me. She moved as if there were lead weights around her ankles.

"You didn't have to come," she said. "It was a long trip for you."

I made an abrupt dismissive motion with my right hand. "I *wanted* to come."

She nodded. Then her face crumpled and she leaned toward me. I caught her and her head fell against my shoulder and she sobbed.

Jack stood a few feet away watching, not interfering but ready to help if need be.

My eyes were wet. I blinked hard and raised my head. The street in front of the church looked wavery and impressionistic through the mist of tears.

I blinked again and my vision cleared. A dark-blue Mercedes 450 SL was parked across the street. My arms tightened around Theresa.

In the front seat of the Mercedes sat Ray Bamford, Shepherd of the Conventicle. He saw me staring at him and he smiled. Oh, how he smiled.

On the ride back to Cambridge, Jack said, "Look, I'll get in touch with the New Hampshire State Police and ask them for a copy of the report on Matt's accident."

I nodded. "Thanks. I just want to know if there's even a remote possibility his car was sabotaged."

"If there is, we'll find out." Jack glanced at me sideways. "You know I thought you were going to storm over to Bamford's car, drag him out of it, and bash his head on the pavement."

"Believe me, I would have if Theresa and Matt's parents hadn't been there. But why put them through a scene like that?"

Jack sighed. "I really don't think Bamford had anything to do with Matt getting killed."

"Then why was he sitting outside the church gloating?"
"Because that's the kind of slime he is."

We drove straight back to Cambridge and got to the police
station in early afternoon. Jack went to the C.I.D. and I went
up to the fourth floor.

For a half-hour I tried to concentrate on my work. But when
I looked at the lined pad I didn't see paper but Ray Bamford's
smiling face. And when I found myself holding the pencil as
if it were a weapon rather than a writing implement, I realized
I wasn't going to accomplish anything creative. I threw the
pencil down hard enough to make it bounce and roll across
the tabletop. I stood up, grabbed my coat from the back of
the chair, and shrugged into it.

Maybe a walk would help settle me. Or at least distract me
from my fantasies of killing Ray Bamford.

The morning's warmth had dissipated into a chill more
characteristic of November in Massachusetts. A fairly stiff
breeze blew in off the river and sent bits and pieces of trash
scuttling along Green Street. It was still sunny, though.

I cut across the municipal parking lot, up Pleasant Street,
and turned left onto Mass. Avenue. I had some vague idea of
spending the next few hours in the Harvard Square bookstores.

I strode along with my head down, my hands deep in my
pockets. As I passed the post office, one of the derelicts who
seem as permanently attached to the place as the sign over the
entrance approached me with the suggestion that I might like
to give him some spare change *and* perform an act of oral
gratification on him. They're not shy, those lads. So vicious
was my responding snarl that he retreated in bug-eyed horror.

I walked past Barsamian's, where people were buying goat
cheese and wild mushroom pizza, and the YWCA, where
some women with all their wordly goods in shopping bags were
waiting for admittance to a room for the night. The contrast

was typical of Central Square. Whole blocks of little bars and
variety stores and lunchrooms had been bulldozed down and
replaced by residential and office condos. The kind that featured concierges and pink marble in the foyer. The only thing
that stayed the same was the people sleeping on the heating
grates outside the buildings.

I never got to the bookstores. A display of hand-thrown
pottery in the window of a crafts shop on the corner of Mass.
Avenue and Trowbridge Street distracted me. A set of six lapis-
tinted goblets in particular drew my eye. There was something
very soothing about that color. I went into the shop to inspect
them at closer range.

At forty bucks apiece, they were a little beyond my means.
No reason I couldn't admire them, of course. And the jug
that went with them, and the serving platter, and the fruit
bowl . . . That teak cheeseboard was awfully nice, too. And
the ceramic-handled fish knives. That Guatemalan hooked
rug would look great on my hearth. Of course at four hundred
dollars it was a bit pricey. What had the Guatemalan peasant
who'd hooked it been paid? Ten cents? Why did you have to
be an investment banker to afford all these simple artifacts of
primitive cultures? I left the shop.

Out on Mass. Avenue the wind was a little brisker and the
temperature a little cooler still. I shivered. Some coffee would
be good. Over the way was an Au Bon Pain. I waited for a
break in the traffic and then hustled across the street.

As I pulled open the restaurant door, I bumped into a tall
bulky figure on his way out of the place. "Excuse me," I said.
He brushed by me without acknowledging the apology. Annoyed, I glanced up at him. And stopped as dead as if I'd hit
a wall.

The tall bulky figure was Alan Sturgis. I turned my head
to watch him as he walked down the street. He still had the
same shambling gait. And the parka he wore looked like a

duplicate of the one he'd had on when he'd been led out of
the courthouse after his sentencing.

I'd only glimpsed his face, but it didn't seem as if prison
had aged him any.

He turned right at the intersection of Mount Auburn and
Mass. Avenue.

What are you standing here like a dummy for? Follow him,
stupid.

He was ambling down Putnam Avenue when I caught up
with him. I stayed about a half a block behind him. Either
he didn't know I was there or he didn't care. At any rate, he
never looked back.

I was sure he'd recognized me when we'd collided. That he
hadn't visibly reacted was typical of him. He'd always behaved
as if he were wrapped in a cloud of unknowing. He'd sat
through his trial and sentencing like a waxworks figure.

I was quite sure his obliviousness was a pretense.

About a quarter of a mile down the street, Sturgis halted in
front of a shop that sold video and computer games and toys.
He inspected the contents of the window and then went inside
the store. I was thirty seconds behind him.

Perhaps he was going to select a little gift for his lady love,
the Arlington librarian. I smiled to myself.

I felt no fear or anxiety pursuing Sturgis like this. I didn't
think he'd assault me in a toy store—even if he *were* the letter
writer, which I doubted. But Fate had handed me the opportunity to check him out, and I'd be a fool not to take it.

For twenty minutes I stood behind a rack of airplane and
ship-model kits and watched Sturgis browse through the stock
of computer games. *Bo-ring.* Finally he selected two and took
them up front to the register. I trailed him at a discreet distance.
I could do that easily—it was a big store.

Sturgis got on line at the checkout counter. I stepped into
one of the cross-aisles so he wouldn't see me. Facing me were

shelves of dolls. Baby dolls, girl dolls, boy dolls, rag dolls, cartoon-character dolls, Barbie dolls, G.I. Joe dolls . . .

Barbie dolls.

Lean, slinky, elegant creatures in a variety of ultra-chic clothes. Blondes. Brunettes. Redheads.

The red-haired doll was wearing a long green gown. Her exotically painted face seemed to leer at me. She was identical to the doll I'd found in my dresser drawer.

I spun around and dashed up the aisle to the register. Sturgis was gone. I ran out of the store and looked up and down Putnam. Nothing.

Slowly, I went back into the toy shop. The clerk at the register gave me a funny look. I smiled at him.

"Do you work here full-time?" I asked.

"I'm the assistant manager."

"Oh. Great. May I ask you a question or two?"

He shrugged. "Shoot."

"The tall guy in the down parka," I said. "The one who just bought the two computer games."

"Yeah?"

"Does he come in here often?"

The assistant manager shrugged again. "I've seen him before."

I nodded. "Has he ever bought anything other than computer stuff?"

The man's eyes narrowed. "Why you want to know?"

I sighed. "It's sort of complicated. I'll be brief. Someone's been sending me anonymous letters and—uh—objects. I have some reason to think that man—his name is Sturgis—might be implicated. What I'd like to know specifically is if he's ever bought a doll. A red-haired doll about a foot tall. The high-fashion kind. This probably would have been some time last month."

The assistant manager pursed his lips in thought, then shook his head. "Can't recall. I don't think so. He never really buys anything but video and computer equipment."

"But if he charged it, you'd have a record of that, wouldn't you? Could you check?"

"That—what did you say his name was?"

"Sturgis."

"Yeah. Well, he always pays in cash."

"Oh," I said, crestfallen.

"But," the assistant manager continued, "let me check the inventory list. That'll tell me if I've sold any of those dolls in the past few weeks."

"Thank you."

He called a clerk who was restocking some shelves with board games to take over at the register. Then he went to the back of the store.

He returned about five minutes later. "I've sold three of those redheaded dolls in the past four weeks. Two were to charge customers. Not Sturgis."

"Who?"

He eyed me for a moment. Then he said, "A woman with a Connecticut address. The other a woman who lives out in Waltham. I'm not telling you their names."

"Sure. Who bought the third doll?"

"I have no idea."

"What?"

"It was a cash transaction."

There were probably a half-a-zillion stores in the greater Boston area that carried those redheaded dolls. That a shop Alan Sturgis frequented carried them most likely meant nothing at all.

Even if the doll that had ended up in my dresser drawer *had* been purchased at the Putnam Avenue store, Sturgis hadn't necessarily been the one to buy it.

Still . . .

When I got back to the police station, I went to the C.I.D. rather than the fourth floor. Jack wasn't alone in his office. With him was a tall, thin, balding man in a rumpled gray suit. What hair he had left was the color of his suit. So, for that matter, was his skin.

"Oops," I said. "Excuse me." I started to withdraw.

"Wait a minute, wait a minute," Jack said. "I was just about to go looking for you." He tilted his head at the man in the gray suit. "Liz, this is Sergeant Roger Delcourt from the Boston Police Department. Roger, Liz Connors."

I smiled. "How do you do?" I offered my hand. Delcourt looked a little startled by the gesture, but, after a second, he held out his own hand. Funny how some men don't think it's quite appropriate to shake with a woman.

"What's up?" I said.

"Sit down," Jack said.

I took the visitor's chair in front of the desk.

"Roger came out to talk to me about a homicide he's investigating," Jack said.

I raised my eyebrows.

"We had a bad one last night," Delcourt said.

I wasn't sure what I was supposed to reply to that, so I kept silent.

"Victim had his throat slit and his chest sliced open," Delcourt said. "Somebody cut out his heart."

"Jesus Christ," I said, recoiling.

"My sentiments exactly," Jack replied. He looked at Delcourt. "Tell her who the victim was."

"Albert Johnson," Delcourt said.

For just the barest second, I drew a blank on the name. It was, after all, a common one. Then I remembered.

"Oh, God," I said.

"Uh-huh," Jack said.

"Chief witness for the prosecution in the Wee Willie Walters case," Delcourt said.

None of us needed the reminder.

Delcourt left a few moments later. Jack called Cassie Stewart at the DA's office. I listened to his side of the conversation. Or, rather, argument.

Jack replaced the telephone receiver back in its cradle, not gently. "God*damnit*," he said, bitterly.

"She won't take the protection," I said. "Even from a female officer?"

"No."

"Will she at least go to a hotel?"

"She said she'd think about it."

I bit my lip. "Why does she think she has to prove that she's tough? We all know she is already." I looked at Jack. "Does she at least have a gun, I hope?"

"Yeah."

"Well, that's something."

"Albert Johnson had a gun. Didn't help him much, did it?"

At five-thirty, Jack, Detective Bobby St. Germain, Detective Artie Lorenzo, Sam Flaherty, and I were sitting at the bar in Frank's Steak House on Mass. Avenue in North Cambridge. Lorenzo and St. Germain were drinking Cokes. I had a vodka martini. Jack had bourbon.

We were talking about what had happened to Albert Johnson.

Jack and I were at loggerheads.

"Look," I said. "Isn't it at least possible that whoever killed Johnson and might try to kill Cassie isn't the guy who wants to kill me? Hell, we don't even know that whoever hacked up Johnson is the same person who wants to get Cass. All three could be totally unrelated."

"That," Jack said, "is stretching coincidence a little further than I'm willing to."

Lorenzo was eating peanuts, one by one, from a bowl on the table. He nodded agreement with Jack.

I looked at St. Germain. He smiled and said, "My book, the odds seem to favor all three being connected."

"Yeah." I sipped my martini.

"Look, Liz," Jack said. "I know how you feel about Hibley. And if it weren't for the second threat against Cass, and Johnson getting chopped up, I'd agree with you that Hibley's the one after you. But . . ." He shook his head. "Things are different now."

"You think Willie Walters ordered Johnson's execution?" I said. "And Cass's? And mine? From prison?"

"Liz, he could be on the moon and still control that gang of his. They're loyal to him. Fanatically loyal. Plus they're a pack of homicidal crazies."

I nodded.

"And you yourself," Jack continued, "once pointed out that Willie is the vengeful type."

"I know I did. I also once pointed out to you that a bad guy with vengeance on his mind would probably go after the judge who sentenced him and the jurors who convicted him before he'd get around to disposing of the writer who wrote about him. Logically, I should be pretty far down on Willie's hit list."

"Why bring logic into it at this point?" Jack said. "This whole thing has been irrational from the word go. As *you* have also pointed out a number of times. Anyway, only God and Willie know what Willie's priorities are."

Lorenzo and St. Germain looked studiously at their Cokes. I could understand why. Jack and I were bordering on having a fight, or at least we sounded as if we were, and it must have been an uncomfortable thing for them to witness. He was their superior officer.

The same thought probably passed through Jack's mind. He took a deep breath and, following that, a sip of bourbon.

"All right," he said. "No need for either of us to get unglued. We got enough problems already."

"Yes."

Lorenzo cleared his throat. I glanced at him. He smiled briefly and then went back to popping peanuts.

St. Germain said, "It's the fact that Johnson had his heart cut out and you got a doll with slash marks on its chest. That's what ties things together."

"Sure."

It wasn't that I couldn't see his and Lorenzo's and Jack's point. I could, perfectly well. Their argument made complete sense.

We all knew Willie, and what a butcher he was. And how his posse would follow his lead.

I, however, was the only one who knew Garrett, and the only one who could imagine what kind of monster *he* might be.

And what about the incident in the toy store this afternoon? I hadn't had a chance to mention that to Jack. Would that alter his thinking?

Flaherty had been quiet throughout the discussion, placidly drinking beer. I looked at him. He shrugged, ate some peanuts, and said, "My money's on Willie."

"Right."

We finished our drinks. Jack paid the check.

On the sidewalk outside Frank's he and I said goodnight to the other three. Flaherty's car was in the lot behind the restaurant. Lorenzo and St. Germain started walking south on Mass. Avenue. I watched them get into a car parked about a block down the street.

"They didn't have anything alcoholic to drink," I said. "Are they working tonight?"

Jack nodded. "They'll be hanging around outside Cass's. She doesn't know."

"Good."

We walked toward Jack's car.

"You mad at me still?" he asked.

"No," I said. "I never was."

We made a stop at my place to check my mail and the answering machine. There were no dead dolls in the dresser drawer, nor in the meat keeper of the refrigerator, nor indeed anywhere else. No threats scrawled in blood on the living room walls. There was, however, a phone message from Brandon Peters, the editor of *Cambridge Monthly*. He wanted me to call him ASAP, at home if I couldn't get him at the magazine office.

It was well after six. I called him at home.

"Liz," he said. "Good to hear from you."

"And you. What's up?"

There was a little silence on the other end of the line. Then he said, "Well, probably nothing, really."

"What is it, Brandon?"

"Liz, I really liked the article you did for me about Murray Evans. Great stuff."

"Thank you."

"The thing is, some of our readers didn't like it."

I said, "So what else is new?"

"Yeah, yeah," he replied. "I know. We're always getting letters saying things like, *How could you print such trash,* or *Please cancel my subscription to your salacious rag immediately,* or *I must take issue with the totally one-sided picture you presented of* . . . hey, every magazine gets letters like that every month about every article they run. Right?"

"Uh-huh," I said, wishing he'd get to the point.

"Okay," Peters said. "Look, the thing is, some of the mail we've been getting in response to the Murray Evans piece is—"

"A little weirder than usual?" I interrupted.

"You got it."

"Go on," I said.

"All right. Now, let me first tell you that some of the letters have been complimentary."

"Good."

"Okay. And some have been critical. But, you know, *rationally* critical."

"Mm-hmm."

"It's the third batch that bothers me."

"Yes?"

"All of them are anonymous."

"Well, that in itself isn't terribly unusual, is it?"

"No. But these . . . they're personal attacks on *you*, Liz."

"I see."

"I have a couple here. You want me to read them to you?"

"Yes."

"Okay."

I heard a faint rattling noise. Paper being unfolded.

"All right, here's one that goes on at some length about what a fine doctor and general swell human being Murray Evans is, and how his conviction was a tragic miscarriage of justice and all that. Then it goes on to call you vile and vicious for having perpetuated all the lies about him. Here's the exact quote: *Elizabeth Connors truly shows herself to be both vile and vicious in her libelous account of Dr. Evans's travail.*"

"*Travail?*" I said. "Heavy."

"Yeah, okay, that letter is one of the milder ones. Here we have another that refers to you as a *lying bitch* and another that calls you a *vindictive bitch* . . . I mean, doesn't that strike you as a little extreme?"

"Yes," I said. "It does. Brandon, look. May I have those letters?"

"What the hell you want them for?"

"I want to compare them with some anonymous hate mail I've been getting at home."

"Jesus. Stuff like this?"

"There's a certain similarity."

"Jesus," he repeated. "Well, sure you can have them. Of course."

"Good. I'll pick them up at the office tomorrow."

"Sure. Could you make it late in the afternoon, though?"

"No problem."

"Okay. See you then. And, Liz . . ."

"What?"

"These letters you've been getting at home. Are any of them, uh, threats?"

"How did you guess?"

"I hope you're watching your ass."

"I am."

"Okay. 'Bye."

Jack had come over to stand beside me and listen to my end of the conversation. I hung up the phone and stared at him.

"What is it?" he asked.

I told him.

"Didn't Evans have character witnesses at his trial?" Jack said, when I'd finished.

I nodded. "A whole parade of them. All testifying to his sterling character and irreproachable conduct. Some of them were even patients of his—the young, affluent ones—some were his golf buddies, some were people who'd worked with him on various charity committees. All credible people. They were all horrified that anyone could even imagine that a pillar of the community like dear Murray might be sexually assaulting his elderly Medicare patients."

"So maybe it's one of them—one of the character witnesses—who's writing the hate mail to *Cambridge Monthly*."

I nodded again, a little wearily. "And maybe it's the same person who's been sending letters to me. And photos with the eyes burned out."

Jack looked at me for a moment. Then he put his hand on my shoulder. "Come on," he said. "Let's go to my place and feed the dog and feed ourselves."

I had a new book on crime investigation techniques I wanted to read, and I made a real effort to do so after dinner. But when I found myself rereading the same page three times and not absorbing any of its contents, I quit. I closed the book and set it on the end table by the couch.

I put my head back against the cushions and shut my eyes. The conversation I'd had earlier with Brandon Peters ran through my mind.

The letters he'd quoted me were almost certainly from the pens of the die-hard supporters of Murray Evans. Not necessarily one of his character witnesses. He'd had many other friends and colleagues on his side. They had in fact packed the courtroom throughout his trial.

After the verdict had been handed down, one of this genteel horde, a fellow physician and squash player, had been interviewed by a reporter for a local television station. He called Evans's conviction "a terrible, tragic miscarriage of justice."

Big, good-looking Murray. He had certainly learned well the art of commanding blind loyalty.

How far would his allies go to show their support?

Suppose, when I picked up the letters from Peters tomorrow, I found that they were printed in pencil on cheap white generic paper. Like the ones I'd gotten? What would we intuit from that?

At 9:00 P.M., the phone rang. Jack went to answer it. I was lying on the couch, flipping through the November issue of *Vanity Fair*. I couldn't concentrate on it any more than the book I'd set aside earlier. When Jack came back to the living room, I looked up at him. There was a tightness to his face around the eyes that I recognized.

"Something?" I said, tossing the magazine aside.

"That was Lorenzo," Jack said. "Cass hasn't been home all evening. Her place is dark."

I lay quietly for a second, then pushed myself into a sitting position. "Maybe she took your advice and went straight to a hotel."

He nodded.

"Or maybe she had a date right after work and didn't bother to go home to change."

"Maybe."

We stayed up till midnight. We read, and watched the eleven o'clock news. It sucked, as usual. The phone stayed silent.

It rang again at 2:00 A.M. We both must have been sleeping lightly, because we woke quickly and simultaneously. Jack fumbled the receiver off the hook in the middle of the second ring. "Yeah?" he said.

I brushed my hair back and massaged my face.

"Oh, *shit*," Jack said. "Ah, God. No." A moment later: "All right. I'll be there in fifteen minutes. Who's there now? Yeah. Okay. Uh-huh." He hung up the phone and turned on the night-table lamp. He threw back the bed covers. I blinked.

"Get dressed," he said. "We have to go."

"Go where?" I said muzzily. "What is it?"

"Cassie's dead," he said.

I made a noise in the back of my throat.

"Come on," he snapped. "Get up and get dressed. I can't leave you here alone now." He grabbed his jeans from the back of the chair as I scrambled out of bed.

I splashed some cold water on my face, combed my hair haphazardly, and bundled into slacks, a cotton turtleneck, and heavy wool sweater. I snatched my windbreaker from the hall coat rack as we went to the front door.

In silence, we left the house. The night was very cold and dark. And still. Our footsteps were soundless as we hurried down the path to the driveway.

In the car, going down Mass. Avenue, I broke the silence.

"I know you don't have details yet," I said. "But . . . what . . . how did it happen?"

"About a half an hour ago," Jack said. "One of the cruisers was on Commercial Avenue. And they saw a car with its headlights on outside the Cambridgeside Galeria parking garage. They went to check it out. It was Cass's car." Jack took a deep breath. "Cass was in the front seat."

"Dead."

"Apparently of multiple stab or slash wounds to the chest. Her throat was slit."

I squeezed my eyes shut.

"It was hard for them to tell, exactly," Jack said. "There was so much blood. The front seat was swimming in it. When they opened the car door, it came out like a waterfall."

At two-thirty in the morning, the Galeria lot was always empty. Not this morning. When we arrived, there were three Cambridge Police blue-and-whites, two unmarked Cambridge detectives' cars, what I supposed were some state police investigative unit cars, and an ambulance. The medical examiner was present. So were the forensics people and the police photographer. So was someone from the District Attorney's office.

Whoever that last was had been one of Cass's colleagues. Maybe even a friend.

As we pulled up to the garage entrance, so did another two unmarked cars. More detectives.

Lights had been set up to illuminate the immediate area. It looked like some kind of grotesque movie set.

Jack parked next to one of the Cambridge cruisers. We got out of the car. In the artificial light, his face was the color of yellow chalk.

"I don't think you want to see this," he said. "I don't want to see it." He walked away, toward a group of detectives.

No, I didn't want to see it, but something compelled me to move closer.

Cass's car was a red Toyota Camry. The front driver's side door was open. On the pavement was a huge glistening puddle like an oil slick. The blood was a darker black than the pavement.

I heard a slight noise to my left. I turned my head. About ten feet away from me stood Bobby St. Germain. His hands were shoved into his jacket pockets and his shoulders were hunched. He stared straight ahead of him.

I wasn't sure, but I thought he might be crying.

10

It was eleven the next morning, and Jack and I were in his office. My eyes were gritty, and I had the dull headache that comes from insufficient sleep. Jack looked like I felt. He had just come back from two hours of questioning people who had had contact with Cassie yesterday.

I reached for my coffee. "What did you find out?" I asked.

He rubbed his face with both hands. "I was able to backtrack her movements."

"Oh?" I took a sip of coffee.

"You were right," Jack said. "She had a date after work. To meet an old law-school friend for a drink, dinner, and movie. She went straight from the courthouse, apparently. Left at ten after five and met the friend in the bar of the Ritz-Carlton at five-thirty. They had two drinks apiece, then walked down Newbury Street to the Italian place, Via Veneto, for dinner. Finished dinner at eight-thirty, then walked over to the theater on Boylston to catch the nine o'clock show. Movie let out at ten of eleven. They went for a cappuccino. Then back to Cassie's car, and Cassie drove the friend home to Dorchester. Said goodnight at twelve-thirty and, as far as the friend knows, headed back home to Cambridge."

"Who's the friend?"

"A woman who's an ADA for Suffolk." Jack rubbed his face again.

I shook my head. "Did you have to break the news to her?"
He nodded.

I grimaced. There were parts of his job I envied him, but not that one. I took another sip of coffee.

"The friend's not a suspect, is she?" I asked.

Jack let his hands drop from his face and looked at me sharply. "Not at this point."

I got up, went over to the window, and looked out at Green Street. "You really like one of Wee Willie Walters's boys for this, don't you?"

"For doing what was done to Cass? Yes, I do."

"And me?"

"I think Willie's the strongest possibility there, too. After what happened last night, even stronger."

"But you don't think Willie wrote those letters to *Cambridge Monthly.*"

"Off the top of my head, no. But I want to see them, anyway."

"Garrett could have written them."

Jack took a deep breath. "Yes, maybe he could have. And maybe the person who sent both sets of letters—to you and to the magazine—and sent you the photo with the burned-out eyes and put the doll in your dresser drawer isn't Hibley or one of Walters's boys or one of Evans's character witnesses. Or even Dorothy Evans. Or Alan Sturgis. Maybe we're both barking up the wrong tree. Maybe it's one fucking psycho who got Cass and another who's after you, and we never heard of either one of them. *I don't fucking know.* I go on the odds."

I closed my eyes and shook my head slightly, not agreeing, yet not disagreeing.

All I was sure of was that this was no time for Jack and me to be fighting with each other.

When would this end?

Maybe a better question was, *how* would this end?

The phone rang. While Jack spoke to whoever it was, I tried to organize my thoughts.

I was willing to buy that Wee Willie Walters had ordered the slaughter of Cass and Albert Johnson.

But not of me.

Sure, Cass and I had received similar-sounding threats. Hers had come by phone rather than by letter, though.

And hers—the second one, anyway—had been in the plural. *We're* going to kill you, the caller had said.

The voice in the letters to me had been singular. And soon *I'll* come to kill you.

A meaningless distinction?

I didn't pose it to Jack.

He left to go to the courthouse to confer with the state police detectives. I trudged upstairs to the fourth floor, taking a fresh cup of coffee with me. The desktop in my cubbyhole was littered with the manuscript pages of the short story I was supposed to be writing. I looked at the disarray for a moment. Then I put down the coffee cup, gathered all the pages together in a neat pile, and set them aside. I wasn't going to kid myself that I'd get any work done today.

It was good I was tired. Otherwise, I'd have run around the police station punching holes in the walls out of frustrated fury at my own helplessness.

More for something to do than anything else, I went out an hour later to get the papers at the tobacconist-newsdealer-porn bookstore on the corner of Mass. Avenue and Western. Since Cassie's death had occurred well after press time, neither the *Globe* nor the *Herald* carried articles about it. I was sure they would make up for that lack tomorrow.

The killing of Albert Johnson was covered briefly by each paper. Both accounts described Johnson merely as the victim of a stabbing. Apparently the Boston police had withheld the gorier details of his murder.

I wondered how long it would be before some enterprising reporter ferreted them out.

And when someone would notice the similarity between the method used to execute Johnson and that used to execute Cassie.

I remembered the first time I'd interviewed Cass for the Wee Willie Walters article. We'd met for drinks at Ryle's on Hampshire Street. I'd gotten there first. When she'd walked in, ten minutes late, the whole place had stopped what it was doing to watch her cross the room.

My brain felt like my nephew Bobby's Play-Doh when he left it out overnight and it all dried into crumbly pink and blue and yellow bits. My thoughts darted here and there.

Why hadn't I received any mail at the police station or at Jack's recently? The campaign seemed to have stopped with the charred-eyes photo.

What was it the final letter had said?

The countdown is beginning.

Did that mean the letter-writer felt I'd been sufficiently warned of what was to come? Or had he given up on me and turned his attention elsewhere?

Speaking of letters, Teddy Byrne, the Arlington cop, had promised to get back to Jack right away if the anonymous notes the reference librarian was receiving turned threatening. So far they seemed to be only . . . wistful.

There was no guarantee, Byrne thought, that they'd stay innocuous. In his view, their author was seriously disturbed.

Two of the letters the librarian had received had been printed on plain paper. Unfortunately, she'd thrown them into the trash after reading them, so there was no way of telling whether the paper was the same cheap white stock my letter-writer had used.

The third and fourth letters she'd saved and given to Teddy Byrne. They'd been typed on a computer. A top-of-the-line model. Why the switch, I wondered.

* * *

It occurred to me—belatedly, but in the past eighteen hours or so I hadn't been too quick on the uptake—that maybe I should get the librarian's name and call her. We could, literally, compare notes.

Not today. My mind was too fuzzy.

Tomorrow, after a good night's sleep. If I could get one. Then I'd make the call.

Fogged as my brain was, it had no trouble conjuring the image of Alan Sturgis. Big and bulky, he moved like a displaced mastodon onto the center stage of my consciousness. And stood there in his chinos and down parka.

That vision was almost immediately supplanted by a ludicrous one of Sturgis hotly pursuing the reference librarian through the stacks of the Arlington library.

With what enticements had Supernerd the Computer Jockey tried to court his lady love? *Hey, babe, come up to my place and I'll show you my spread sheets.*

Actually, it wasn't all that funny. It could be damned dangerous for the librarian.

Sturgis was, to the best of my knowledge, a guy who'd never had a romantic or long-term sexual relationship with a woman, not just throughout his adolescence, but through his college and working years as well. Perhaps there had been some hasty interludes here and there with a prostitute or a pickup.

Certainly Allenwood hadn't offered him much opportunity to form a liaison. Not with a woman, anyway. And I had no reason to think Sturgis was gay.

Okay, say the librarian was the first female on whom Sturgis had ever focused his adult passions. Her response had been to reject him out of hand. Not only that, but then to turn on him and report him to the police. How had all that made him feel?

And how had he felt when he read the article another

woman had written about him? The one in which I'd quoted people who'd described him as "a bore" and "a nerd"?

Not good, I would think. Probably really bad.

Of course, he'd read my article before he'd gone after the reference librarian. Or so I assumed.

Maybe that made me the cause of what he was doing now. Maybe he thought so too.

It was only then that I remembered I *still* hadn't told Jack about the episode in the Putnam Avenue toy store.

Even as an infant, I was never able to sleep in the daytime, which was okay with my mother but which pissed the hell out of my nurse. It must have been a measure of my exhaustion, then, that I dozed off in my cubbyhole that afternoon, following a brief and dispirited lunch with the woman who worked in the crime analysis bureau.

I was slumped over the desk with my head resting on my folded arms when someone shook my shoulder. I jumped slightly, blinked, and looked up. Jack was standing beside me.

"Oh, hi," I said. I shoved myself away from the desk and fell back into the chair. I yawned and shook my head. "What time is it?"

"Almost four."

I sat bolt upright. "My God, I have to get to the magazine office and get those letters from Peters."

"Yeah." Jack held out to me a large, fatly stuffed manila envelope. I took it.

"What's this?"

"Plastic folders for the letters."

"Oh. Right. Excuse me."

I got up and went to the ladies' room across the hall from the radio room. I combed my hair. My reflection in the mirror over the sink was ghastly. Strictly Grendel's mom. I dabbed on a little blusher and lip gloss. Grendel's younger sister.

Jack was waiting for me in the hall. He held my jacket and the manila envelope.

"Two of the detectives will give you a hitch over to the magazine," he said. "They're riding around that sector today anyway."

"Oh. Good. Which two?"

"Mike and Gloria."

I nodded. "Fine."

As we went down the stairs, I handed Jack the envelope so I could shrug into my jacket.

"How's the investigation going?" I said.

He made a face. I took the envelope back from him.

When we got to the third-floor landing, the captain of detectives was standing outside the doors to the C.I.D. He gave me a brief smile and said to Jack, "Gotta see you for a minute."

"Sure." Jack touched my arm. "Can you wait here for me for a bit? If I'm not out in five minutes, go ahead down to the parking lot and meet Mike and Gloria."

"Okay."

He followed the captain into the C.I.D. I sat down on the wooden bench in the corridor, next to a squirmy-looking kid in his late teens.

I crossed my legs and rested the manila envelope in my lap. The kid next to me continued to fidget.

"You a lawyer?" he blurted.

Startled, I gave him a sharp glance. "No."

"Oh." He looked away from me.

Amused, I wondered how desperately he thought he needed counsel.

"Cop wants to see me," he said, as if reading my thoughts. "I didn't do nothing."

I was entertaining myself trying to figure out whether this was the 3878th or 3879th time I'd heard a suspect or felon speak those exact same words when Jack came through the double doors. I rose and we started down the stairs.

Jack's face had that tight-around-the-eyes expression.

"What is it?" I said.

We were on the second-floor landing, outside the chief's office and the crime analysis bureau.

"The judge in the Wee Willie Walters case just got a death threat."

I'm not even going to try to think about this now, I decided as I continued down the stairs. I can't.

Mike Sanguedolce and Gloria Pacheco were waiting for me in the police parking lot on Green Street. They were sitting in a ten-year-old Dodge Dart that had probably originally been silver. Now it was dull gray with attractively contrasting rust trim.

I slid into the back seat. "Some set of wheels the department gives you people to ride around in."

"Don't knock it," Sanguedolce said. "The chop shop guys see it and run in the opposite direction holding their noses."

Gloria was bent forward, feeling around beneath the front seat. "Where the hell's the blue light gone to?" she said.

"It was here an hour ago," Mike said.

"I bet Lorenzo stole it for his heap," Gloria complained. She sat up, tossing back her hair. "He's always doing that."

"Well, what the hell are we supposed to do if we have to chase a bad guy?" Mike said.

Gloria looked at him. "I'll hang my head out the window and make siren noises."

"Right," Mike said. He started the car.

I held up both index fingers. "One, two, three, four," I said. "All together, now . . ."

In chorus, the three of us chanted the line that every Cambridge police officer spoke before starting on his or her rounds: "Let's go catch some crooks."

We wheeled out of the parking lot.

Gloria said something to Mike about having to go to court tomorrow to pick up an arrest warrant. Mike grumbled back at her about his own appointments.

I leaned back against the seat and closed my eyes, half-listening to their talk. And their banter. That the two of them could kid around in view of what had happened to Cassie, to one of their own, this morning—and Mike and Gloria had been two of the detectives responding to *that* scene—might have surprised anyone who didn't know cops the way I did.

The joking was how they kept sane.

Me too.

The police radio burbled softly.

"Liz," Mike said.

I opened my eyes. "Ya?"

"We'll take you to your magazine place first, okay?"

"Sure, if it's not trouble."

"None at all," Gloria said. "We'll wait for you."

"Oh, you don't have to do that."

She smiled. "Sure we do."

"Waiting doesn't make no nevermind to us anyway," Mike said. "It's one of our best things."

I laughed. "Okay."

Cambridge Monthly had recently moved its offices from a cruddy hole on the fifth floor of a building on Inman Street to a truly fabulous suite in a hi-tech monolith in Kendall Square. I liked the old place better.

Mike pulled up in front of the monolith and stopped in a tow zone.

"I'll be as quick as possible," I promised, getting out of the car.

"Don't rush," Gloria said.

The *Cambridge Monthly* office was on the building's eighth floor. The elevator I took up there was a marvel of speed and silence. Probably designed by an M.I.T. freshman as an entry in the school science fair. The g-force clogged my ears.

Marianne, the magazine's receptionist, told me to go straight in to Peters's office. I did.

Everything about Brandon Peters was thin—body, face, hair, and, very often, skin. As I entered his office, he rose from behind his desk and came forward to give me a kiss on the cheek.

"We got another one today," he said.

I raised my eyebrows.

He went back to his desk and rummaged around for a moment. From the litter on the blotter he picked out a sheet of paper. Holding it by the corner, he passed it over to me.

Before I read it, I slipped it into one of the plastic folders Jack had given me. Which was sort of like locking the barn door after the horse had been stolen, in view of the fact that the letter had been handled by Peters, Marianne, the mailroom people, and God knew who else.

It was written on pink stationery in loopy script. It said: "Murray Evans is a fine man. Something bad should happen to Elizabeth Connors for what she wrote about him."

There were five more letters. I put each one in its own plastic folder.

Three were typed—not, as far as I could tell, on the same machine. One was handwritten in a large, rounded backhand with circles dotting the "i's." The fifth was printed. The print was squarer than that of the eight letters I'd received.

There was, however, a distinct commonality of wording in all the letters. Three times I was described as "vile," twice as "vicious." Four times as a "lying bitch." Once as a "vindictive bitch."

It had a familiar resonance. The first two letters I'd received at home had called me a "vicious bitch."

I stuffed the plastic folders back into the envelope and got up to leave.

"Brandon," I said, "thanks for keeping these for me. You wouldn't happen to have the envelopes they came in, would you? I'd like to see the postmarks."

"Oh, shit," he said, staring at me. "Marianne threw them away. I should have told her . . . damn. I'm sorry."

I shook my head. "Probably won't matter in the long run. Thanks again."

He nodded.

"Well, good-bye."

When I was at the door, he said, "Liz."

"Yes?"

"Like I said the other night, be careful."

"Of course."

"You're my best writer. I can't afford to lose you."

When all this was over, he'd probably want me to do a piece for him on the experience.

I probably would.

"That was quick," Gloria said, as I got into the car. She looked at me over the top of the front seat. "What were they like?"

"The letters?" I handed her the envelope. "You're a detective. See for yourself."

Mike started the car and pulled out of the tow zone. "You hear about the threat on Judge Rusher?"

"Jack told me about it just before I met you two."

Gloria was absorbed in the contents of the envelope.

"Buncha sickos," she mumbled. I assumed she was referring to the author, or authors, of the letters.

"Did you see the ones I got at my place and Jack's and the station?" I asked.

She nodded. "Jack showed them to me." She wrinkled her nose. "Scary." She patted the folder in her lap. "These don't look like them, though. I mean, in terms of the handwriting."

"Sentiments are similar," I said.

She nodded.

The radio said something through a crackle of static. Mike picked it up and raised it to his face. "Forty-eight," he said into the transmitter. "We're in the vicinity. We'll swing by there." He set the radio back on the car seat. Gloria scooped up the plastic folders and slipped them into the envelope.

"What do we have?" she said to Mike.

"Some kind of a disturbance in the lobby of the Marriott."

"Serious?"

He shrugged. "Doesn't sound like a blue light special." Over his shoulder, he said to me, "You want to come with us while we check it?"

I thought for a moment. "Yeah, why not?"

"Okay. We'll drop you at the station afterward."

Mike turned the car onto Broadway. Gloria didn't bother cranking down the window and making siren noises, I noted.

It was a quarter to five now, and almost completely dark. The new buildings were beautifully lit. Remember the "Tomorrowland" episodes on *Disneyland* in the late fifties and early sixties? I always did when I was in Kendall Square. It was that kind of ethereal-futuristic.

We pulled into the circular drive before the rear entrance to the Marriott. Mike stopped the car and the three of us got out. Gloria winked at me. "Ready to do some *real* police work?" she said.

"Absolutely."

We walked into the hotel lobby. Mike identified himself to the doorman. The doorman nodded and picked up his house phone. A moment later, a man in a dark suit came hurrying toward us. On the outer breast pocket of his suit coat was pinned a tag that read "Assistant Manager."

The lobby looked like a giant living room: strategically placed groupings of couches, chairs, and occasional tables with lamps and ceramic vases on them. To the right was the registration desk. To the left was a small, elegant bar, now closed.

Someone had apparently hurled or knocked one of the vases to the marble floor. A woman in a white uniform was picking up the pieces and putting them in a cloth trash bag.

"We can't get rid of her," the assistant manager was saying. "One of the bellboys tried to restrain her and she kicked him. She came in here and started screaming and accosting the guests. Then"—he tilted his head in the direction of the wreckage of the vase—"she tried to throw that at the desk." He shook his head. "I don't know whether she's drunk or on drugs or crazy or what."

"Where is she now?" Gloria asked.

"In the main bar," the assistant manager replied.

We followed him out of the lobby and down a short hall. Behind his back, Gloria and Mike were rolling their eyes at each other.

"You want to bet me it's Bettina?" Gloria said in a low voice.

"No," Mike said. "I'd lose."

The main bar was a huge room built on three levels. On the wall farthest from us hung a row of giant TV screens, all showing the same rock video. The music was loud.

Not so loud, however, that over it we couldn't hear the screech of a female voice.

"Fuckin' assholes get away from me I'll kill ya fuckin' asshole fuckers get away cocksuckers."

Gloria sighed. "Bettina." She looked at Mike. "I'll call for the wagon." She dug in her purse for her radio.

We passed a knot of wide-eyed waitresses and walked toward the service area.

A thin young woman with wildly snarled shoulder-length black hair sat on the floor with her legs straight out before her and her back pressed against the bar. She wore a green sweater with holes in it and ragged jeans. On her feet were stained white sneakers. The sole of one was coming away from the upper.

Her eyes were half-closed and she rolled her head from side to side. The obscene litany continued to spew from her lips.

The bar stools around her had been knocked on their sides. The customers who'd been at the bar now stood in a semicircle fifteen feet away from the woman, staring.

Mike went toward her. Gloria spoke into her radio, clicked it off, and dropped it back into her purse. She walked to the bar to join Mike.

The obscene screeching subsided. I leaned against a brass railing.

Gloria knelt down before the woman and began talking to her in tones inaudible to me. The woman hiccuped. Then she began to weep. Gloria rose, took a fistful of cocktail napkins from the bar, and handed them to her.

Mike wandered over to me.

"Who is she?" I asked. "Other than what she appears to be?"

"Bettina? A real sad case." He shook his head. "When she's off the sauce, she's a sweet kid. Wouldn't hurt a fly."

"She live around here?"

"Over on Spring Street with her parents."

"What's wrong with her beyond the booze?"

"Well, she's not very bright, and she's had emotional problems ever since she was a kid. She's only twenty-three now, believe it or not."

"God."

"Anyhow, she's been institutionalized about a zillion times. Like I said, she's home now. She spends the day on the streets, just wandering around."

I made a "tch" sound.

"She doesn't get out of control that often," Mike said. "Only when some son-of-a-bitch decides it would be funny to get her drunk. She's been gang-banged a few times when she's had a load on."

I winced. "What are you going to do with her now?"

"Lock her up. Notify her folks. Take her to detox. See if the hotel wants to press charges." He shrugged, and looked a little helpless. "There's not a hell of a lot we *can* do."

"I know."

"Wish the wagon would get here," he said.

I looked at my watch. "Mike?"

"Ya?"

"You guys have your hands full. Why don't I give Jack a call and tell him where I am and ask him to pick me up? It's after five. He'll be leaving the station anyway."

"Well . . ."

I smiled. "I know, I know. You're not supposed to let me out of your sight." I pointed in the direction of the lobby. "I'll call from there. Wee Willie Walters or whoever isn't going to leap out from behind the registration desk with a chainsaw."

"All right."

I patted his arm. "Thank you for the ride to the magazine. And your company." I glanced over at Gloria and Bettina. "*And* the chance to do some *real* police work."

He laughed. "You're welcome."

I walked out of the bar to the pay phones. I got a dime from my purse, dropped it into the coin slot, and dialed Jack's number. He answered on the second ring.

"I'm here in the posh Marriott," I said. "Assisting two dedicated law enforcement agents in the performance of their duties."

"Oh, really?" Jack sounded amused. "What's going down?"

"Does the name Bettina ring a bell?"

"Oh, Christ. Let me guess. She went apeshit in the bar, right?"

"You got it. Listen, how'd you like to pick me up here?"

"Sure. Did you get the letters from Peters?"

"Got 'em right with me."

"What're they like?"

"I'll show you. As long as we're in this neighborhood, can I buy you a drink at the M.I.T. Faculty Club?"

"Yes, you can."

"Good. Where shall I meet you? The Main Street entrance to the Marriott?"

"In ten minutes," he said.

We hung up.

As I walked across the lobby I saw two uniformed guys come in the front entrance to the hotel. The police wagon was parked out on Mass. Avenue, its blue lights flashing. The two cops turned right and went down the corridor to the big bar.

Did I have the money to pay for our drinks? I had the funny feeling I didn't.

I stopped and fished my wallet out of my purse. I opened it. Three bucks. Damn.

There was an automatic teller machine on the corner of Warburton Street and Mass. Avenue, about three hundred feet away from the front of the Marriott. I could race over there and get some cash and be back here in five minutes.

If there was a line of people waiting to use the ATM, which there usually was, it would take more than five minutes.

If I wasn't at the entrance to the Marriott when Jack showed up, he'd probably call out the National Guard or something.

I ground my teeth in irritation. Not at Jack. At the present circumstances of my existence.

My entire adult life I'd spent moving freely, going wherever I wanted whenever I felt like it. And although I valued that freedom, I had taken it for granted. It was as natural and as reflexive to me as breathing.

And now I'd lost it.

I threw my wallet back into my purse and stomped toward the rear entrance to the hotel.

I hated waiting anyway. I wasn't a cop.

Warburton Street ran right along in front of the building that housed the M.I.T. Faculty Club. Jack could park his car there. Then he could walk with me to the damn ATM and stand there while I got the damn cash.

Daddy and his baby girl. Shit.

Oh, calm down, I said to myself as I reached the glass doors. This isn't going to last forever.

I heard footsteps behind me and turned quickly. It was Gloria. "Jack just called me on the radio," she said.

I frowned at her. "What's up?"

"Nothing serious. It's just that he's going to be tied up with the captain for another ten or fifteen minutes. He said you should just wait here for him, though, and he'll be along as quickly as possible."

I sighed loudly.

She looked at me with some sympathy. "I know how you feel. I'd be climbing the walls if I were you."

"Gloria," I said. "I only want one thing."

"What's that?"

"When the person who's after me is caught, I want to be locked in a cell with him so I can torture him for about six hours."

She grinned. "Maybe we can arrange it. Hell, I'll even dig up a rubber hose."

The two uniformed cops came through the lobby with Bettina in tow. She had her head down, so that her hair covered her face. They shepherded her out of the front door of the hotel.

Mike appeared. "We're done here," he said. He made a sour face. "The hotel wants to press charges. So does the bellboy she kicked in the balls."

"Gee, I hope he's not permanently incapacitated," Gloria said.

"Why? You want to date him? Come on, let's go." Mike smiled at me. " 'Night, Liz."

I waved to them as they got into the gray car and pulled out of the circular drive. Mike tooted the horn once in response.

I wandered back into the lobby and sat down on one of the couches. I took the bulky manila envelope from beneath my arm and looked at it for a moment. Then I opened it. Might as well kill time by rereading the old fan mail.

The first folder I withdrew contained the letter written in loopy script on pink paper. The one that said that something bad ought to happen to me for saying unkind things about that maligned saint Murray Evans. I would have dearly loved to have known if the envelope it had come in had been postmarked Wellesley.

I figured Dorothy Evans for the kind of woman who'd use shell-pink stationery and have silly-looking handwriting.

I also figured her for the kind of woman who'd use a coy phrase like "something bad" instead of spelling out a more specific threat.

I remembered Dorothy at her husband's trial. The very

image of the loving, supportive spouse, she'd been. The trial had dragged out—five days a week for six weeks—and I hadn't seen her wear the same designer outfit twice. She'd burst into copious tears when the jury had rendered its verdict. Well, she'd had a lot to cry about—there went the Neiman-Marcus and Saks charges right down the toilet.

I looked at the other handwritten letter. The rounded backhand with its circle-dotted "i's" was definitely feminine. Almost exaggeratedly so. I frowned. A man attempting to disguise his script as a woman's? Interesting thought.

The three typewritten letters could be sent to the state police lab, which would be able to determine the makes and models of the three different machines that had been used to produce them. Which wouldn't mean much. One person could have access to three typewriters. Or one to two. Or two to two.

I was studying the printed letter when I realized that I was hearing my name spoken. I dropped the plastic folder. "Elizabeth Connors," a voice flattened by the speaker of a public address system droned, "Elizabeth Connors. Come to the registration area."

I shoved the plastic folders into the manila envelope, rose, and hurried to the desk. A dark-eyed young woman with smooth black hair and coffee-colored skin was flipping through a pile of registration cards. She looked up at me and smiled inquiringly.

"You just paged me," I said. "Elizabeth Connors."

"Oh, yes. You have a phone call." She punched a button on the base of the desk phone, picked up the receiver, and handed it to me.

"Hello," I said.

"Don't sound so worried," Jack's voice replied. "It's only me."

"Where are you?"

"Still in the station. And it looks like I won't be leaving for another hour."

"Why? What's up?"

"I think we've got a break in the investigation."

"Into Cassie's"—I paused and glanced at the woman behind the desk. She wasn't overtly listening to me. Still. "Into what happened last night?" I finished.

"Yeah."

"Oh, that's *great*. A *good* lead?"

"If it pans out."

"*Wonderful*. Listen, why don't I just take a cab or the subway back to the station right now—"

"*No*," Jack said. "Stay where you are."

"But—"

"*No*. Look, this is a tense situation. I don't want to have to worry about you in addition to everything else. Just stay where you are. If I get held up any longer than an hour, I'll send a cruiser for you, okay?"

I was silent for a beat. Then I said, "Jack, exactly how much danger do you think I'm in at this very moment?"

"*I don't know*." His voice was exasperated. "That's why you can't go running around Cambridge by yourself." His voice softened. "Look, cookie, I know what a royal pain in the ass this is for you, but one way or another, it'll probably be over tomorrow."

"Does this have anything to do with Wee Willie Walters?"

"Liz, I can't talk now. I'll explain everything later. Go in the bar and have a drink. I'll find you."

"Yeah," I said. "Later."

" 'Bye."

" 'Bye." I handed the phone receiver back to the registration clerk. "Thank you."

She smiled. "No trouble."

11

I walked back into the lobby, feeling my mouth compress in disgust. I had an urge to take a leaf out of Bettina's book and smash one of the ceramic vases. Not a bad idea, actually. The cops would come and arrest me and take me to the station. On the other hand, I'd seen the women's lock-up, and I preferred not to have to spend the night there being serenaded by drunks and strung-out junkies. The Madonna rock videos in the bar were better musically, though only barely.

Tell me—what ever happened to Ronny and the Daytonas?

I was halfway down the corridor to the bar when I realized anew that I didn't have enough money to buy even one drink.

"Frig it," I said out loud. My voice bounced off the floor and wall. A woman coming out of the ladies' room gave me a surprised look.

I wandered back out into the lobby, feeling like a prisoner. I was ninety-nine point nine percent certain that a trip to the ATM across the street wouldn't jeopardize my life. In any case, I had my handy six-shooter in my purse.

Jack had been quite adamant, though, about me staying put. Be nice to know exactly *why*.

I went into the lobby gift store. Maybe I'd find something there for three dollars or under that would amuse me for the next hour or so.

The gift store sold the usual souvenir crap—Harvard and M.I.T. sweatshirts and mugs—plus an assortment of overpriced clothing, costume jewelry, and toiletries. It also had a newsstand. There was one remaining copy of the *Times*. I grabbed it. Then I glanced over the magazine rack. It held a lot of computer and hi-tech journals.

Magazines like that always made me think of Alan Sturgis. A vision of his tall, bulky form and bland, chubby face rose before me. I wondered idly what he was doing at this very moment. Writing another forlorn mash note to the reference librarian? Or planning to come and kill me?

That latter thought leapt unbidden into my mind. I shook my head as if to dislodge it.

Come on, I said to myself. It was never more than a remote possibility that Sturgis is the guy after you. Despite what Teddy Byrne said about him. Despite what you were thinking this afternoon.

Oh, yeah?

Yes, yeah.

Oh, knock it off.

I paid for the newspaper, went back to the lobby, and found a free chair in which to park myself and read.

I was in the middle of a long article about AIDS research when a voice behind me said, "Liz."

So engrossed was I in my reading that I jumped. Then I whirled around, crumpling the newspaper in my lap.

"I'm sorry; I didn't mean to startle you," Gloria Pacheco said. "Boy, you sure can concentrate."

"What is it?" I said.

She smiled. "Nothing bad. Jack just asked us to pick you up."

"Oh. Okay." I flapped the newspaper and then refolded it. Then I rose and followed Gloria out of the lobby.

The gray and rust car, with Mike Sanguedolce at the wheel, was idling at the curb on Broadway. I got in the back. Mike gave me a brief smile over his shoulder.

"What's happening?" I said.

"What did Jack tell you?" Gloria asked.

I shrugged. "Nothing. Just that there was some kind of hot lead into the investigation of Cassie's death, and that I wasn't allowed to set foot out of the Marriott."

Gloria nodded.

"What's the lead?" I said. "Where did it come from?"

"Informant," Gloria said. "One of the guys in the Dog Posse."

"Oh-ho," I said. "So all of Wee Willie's boys aren't that fanatically loyal to him after all, are they?"

"Not this one, apparently. I don't know the situation, exactly. He probably has some kind of charge hanging over him and figures he can swing a deal for himself with the DA in exchange for informing."

"Sure."

Mike turned the car from Broadway onto Mass. Avenue.

"To make a long story short, this guy gave Jack the name of the guy who killed Cassie and Albert Johnson."

I took a deep breath. "So the two *were* definitely connected."

Gloria looked faintly surprised. "Did you think they weren't?"

"No. But it's good to have it confirmed, isn't it?"

"Anyway," Gloria said, "the informant says this same guy is going to come for Judge Rusher tonight."

"Jesus," I said. "That was quick. He was threatened only this afternoon."

"Yeah." Gloria shrugged.

We turned onto Green Street. Mike stopped the car in front of the police parking lot. "Meet Jack in there," he said. "He's waiting."

I leaned forward and patted his shoulder, then Gloria's. "Okay. Thank you. Have a quiet night."

"Oh, yeah, right," Gloria scoffed.

I left them and went into the parking lot. Jack was standing beside his car.

"I feel like I'm doing the law enforcement shuffle," I said.

He nodded. "Hop in."

I did. "Where are we going?"

"Judge Rusher's."

I looked at him.

"What did Gloria tell you?" he asked.

"That somebody from Willie's gang is supposed to kill Rusher tonight."

"So I've heard."

"Who's the informant?"

"Guy named Jasper St. Vincent."

I thought for a moment. "That name doesn't ring a bell."

"There's no reason why it should. He's a pretty low-level functionary in the gang. I don't think he was even in it, in fact, when Willie was busted."

"Okay," I said, as we pulled out of the parking lot. "Fill in the rest of the blanks for me."

"All right. I got a call this afternoon, about ten minutes after you called me. It was from this St. Vincent."

"Gloria thought he might want to work a deal."

"Yeah, he's got a pretty heavy drug beef hanging over him. Anyway, he gave me the name of the guy who killed Albert Johnson and Cassie and told me also that the same guy was going to take Rusher out sometime tonight."

We were on Western Avenue now, heading toward Memorial Drive.

"Who?"

"Name's Cyprian Lord."

I looked at Jack again, this time in disbelief. "*Cyprian?* A hit man called *Cyprian?* Give me a break. It sounds like one of Oscar Wilde's boyfriends."

Even in the darkness of the car interior, I could see Jack smile. "Yeah, nice, huh? Poetic. But a lot of those cruds have fancy names. Jasper's pretty cute, too."

"Go on."

"Okay, so, according to St. Vincent, Lord *is* acting on instructions from Walters. Those instructions being that Lord is supposed to get rid of everybody who was a major player in Walters's arrest, trial, conviction, sentencing, and, ah, other related people."

"Related people," I repeated. "Like those who gave Walters unfavorable publicity? Media attention? Journalists?"

Jack glanced at me. "St. Vincent didn't name any more names. But . . . yes, I got the impression one or two reporters might be included in the number."

"I see." I looked out the car window at the Harvard houses that lined Memorial Drive. I was remembering what Harry Cummings, the *Globe* reporter, had told me about the posse threats against him. "That's a lot of people Walters wants done away with. Like you, for one. You were a major player in his arrest. But I don't suppose you need the reminder, do you?"

"I haven't been threatened yet."

"The posses aren't shy about killing cops. Either here or in Jamaica. You get in their way and you're gone."

"Thanks, I needed that. Like I've said before, Walters is a law unto himself, honey."

"I'm aware of that."

"The only rules he follows are his own. And those he might change in the middle of the game. Remember this is the guy who chopped up his girlfriend because she burned the dinner." Jack paused. "You know the letter I got, the one that said something about how I could try to protect you, but it wouldn't work in the end?"

"How could I forget it?"

"That always struck me as a Willie letter. As something he

would say. Don't ask me why. It just does. He has that sense of . . . not humor, but—what the hell's the word I'm looking for?"

I shook my head. "You're convinced, then, that it *is* Walters who's after me. Or Lord, acting on Willie's behalf."

Jack glanced at me again. "After what I heard this afternoon, yes. There's more, anyway."

"Than what you've already told me? Let's hear it."

"You know how all the posses dig high-powered weapons, right? Like assault rifles?"

"And nine millimeter handguns," I said. "Just like the one that shot out your living room window. Sure."

"Well, this Lord is proficient with guns. But apparently his weapon of choice is a machete. He's got a thing for knives."

"Uh-huh." Into my mind there sprang the image of the pool of blood beside Cass Stewart's Toyota. Then I had a quick flash of the doll in my dresser drawer. The latter image superimposed itself on the former, like a double-exposure photograph. The doll floated in the red puddle, smiling inanely.

"Lord's got another cute quirk," Jack said.

"What's that?"

"He makes lists of the people he wants to kill. And carries them around with him."

"I see. Jasper St. Vincent told you all this?"

"Uh-huh."

I was silent for a moment. Then I said, "Doesn't it strike you as odd that I've gotten eight threats, Cassie got two, and Rusher only one?"

"Same answer as above," Jack said. "We're dealing with people who operate according to their own weird logic. We've had this conversation before."

"Was Albert Johnson threatened?"

"I don't know."

"Was it Cyprian Lord who sent me the photo with the

burned-out eyes and shot at your house and put the doll in my dresser, do you think? Or someone else in the gang?"

"St. Vincent didn't say. But that doesn't mean much. He didn't know that Cassie or Rusher had been threatened, either. Just about the plan to kill them and . . . whoever else."

We were on Mount Auburn Street now.

"Actually," Jack continued, "I'm not convinced that the burned-eyes photo has anything to do with Walters. *That* I think was sent to you by one of the members of the Murray Evans Fan Club. Maybe by one of the same people who sent the anonymous letters to *Cambridge Monthly*."

I nodded. "Sure have managed to alienate a wide and varied group of people, haven't I?"

He laughed, a note of sympathy in his amusement. "Hazard of your profession, babe."

"Yours too."

"That's the truth."

We turned onto Ash Street. The houses here were large and beautifully maintained, with big manicured lawns. There was an empty parking space in front of a huge white Victorian. Jack backed the car into it.

"Is this where Rusher lives?" I asked.

"Uh-uh," Jack said. "About a block down."

As we were getting out of the car, I said, "You're here to mount guard on Rusher?"

"That's exactly right," Jack said. "He wants protection." He paused a moment and added, "Unlike Cassie."

We walked in silence down the quiet and darkened street for several moments.

"The fact that I'm with you now," I said, "means you think *I'm* in danger tonight as well as Rusher."

"It's not something I care to take chances with," Jack said. "When Lord is locked up, then you can be alone and go places by yourself. What did you think I was going to do—drop you off at my place? I may not be home tonight."

I stopped dead. "Oh, God," I said.

"What?"

"Lucy."

"What about her?"

"She hasn't been out since eight this morning."

"Don't worry," Jack said, impatiently. "I called my landlord. He let her out, fed her, and put the lights on in the apartment."

"Oh. Thank you."

We went up the walk to Judge Rusher's house. It was a three-story building with turrets on either side. A twenties' bootlegger's notion of a medieval fortress. Jack rang the bell. The door was opened by a uniformed policewoman named Linda Marshak. She was a small, slender young woman with reddish-brown hair and pale, freckled skin. I smiled at her as she let us in. We followed her through the foyer and into a divided drawing room that ran from the front to the back of the right side of the building.

Judge Elwood P. Rusher sat in a rocking chair before the fireplace in the rear half of the drawing room. A silver-haired woman in a tweed skirt and cashmere sweater sat diagonally across from him on a chintz-upholstered love seat. The judge rose as Jack and Linda and I entered the room. The woman smiled at us.

Jack and Rusher shook hands. Linda retreated to the foyer. Rusher said to the silver-haired woman, "Marian, this is the young lady who wrote the article about the Walters case."

"How do you do?" I said. "If I'm the one who got us all in this trouble, let me apologize."

"Not your fault," Rusher said brusquely. "Please, sit down."

Jack and I perched on a camelback sofa opposite the Rushers.

Rusher was a heavyset man in his early sixties, with a high-colored, fleshy face and a mass of thick and sculptured-looking white hair. Marian Rusher was thin, with a narrow, fine-featured face.

"Tell me," Judge Rusher said to Jack.

Jack repeated what he'd told me in the car about Jasper St. Vincent and Cyprian Lord. Both Rushers listened very quietly and very attentively. When Jack had finished speaking, Rusher said, "And this Cyprian Lord? Who is he?"

"Like everyone else in the Dog Posse, somebody very dangerous, Judge," Jack said. "He's never been arrested in Cambridge. He has a long record in Boston. Several ADWs, two attempted murder charges, numerous drug arrests."

"Any convictions?" Rusher asked sharply.

Jack shook his head. Marian Rusher clicked her tongue softly.

"According to my informant," Jack said, "Lord is extremely violent and unstable."

"Not unusual for one of the Dog Posse," Rusher said.

"Lord more so than the others," Jack said.

"What a curious name," Mrs. Rusher said. "Dog Posse."

Jack smiled at her briefly. "All the Jamaican gangs refer to themselves as posses. They got the idea from Westerns and TV shows."

Mrs. Rusher's eyes widened. "How extraordinary."

Jack nodded. "The Shower Posse calls itself *shower* because they eliminate their rivals or enemies by *showering* them with bullets."

Mrs. Rusher seemed to shiver. I couldn't blame her.

"Well," Rusher said heavily, "what can we expect to take place this evening?"

"Nothing dramatic, I hope," Jack said. "There's a pickup order out for Lord." He reached into his inside suit pocket and took out a white envelope. He opened it and removed a strip of three black-and-white photographs. "We know what he looks like. Boston gave us these." Jack handed me the photographs. I stared at them.

Cyprian Lord was a medium-skinned black man in his late twenties or early thirties. His eyes were large and thick-lidded and his jaw and cheekbones well cut. A broad straight nose. Rather a good-looking man. Not my image of a crazed assassin. I passed the photographs over to the Rushers.

"We have three undercover units patrolling this neighborhood right now," Jack said. "Officer Marshak and I will be in the house with you. There are people on foot outside."

Judge Rusher nodded. Marian Rusher said, "Thank you."

"Do you mind if I look around at your doors and windows?" Jack asked.

"Of course not," Rusher said. "I'll show you."

"Thanks." Jack stood up. "Linda," he called.

The uniformed policewoman appeared in the drawing-room archway. "Lieutenant?"

Jack gestured at me and Mrs. Rusher. He left the room with the judge. Linda Marshak remained. She was there, I realized, to prevent either the judge's wife or me from getting up and wandering off somewhere. I smiled at Mrs. Rusher and she smiled back. Nobody said anything.

I noticed for the first time that this half of the drawing room had no windows. No wonder we were stationed here.

If things got boring, I figured we could always do dramatic readings of my hate mail.

After about fifteen minutes, Jack and Judge Rusher returned to the drawing room. Jack smiled at Linda and she left. Judge Rusher settled in the rocking chair. Jack stood before the fireplace, his hands in his pockets.

"Can you tell me again about the threat you received this afternoon?" Jack asked.

Rusher nodded. "It was a little after three-thirty. I was in my chambers; the phone rang. When I picked it up, a man's voice, slight Jamaican accent, said, 'We gonna come for you real soon, whitemeat motherfucker.' "

"That's all?" Jack said.

"That's all."

Marian Rusher reached out and placed her right hand over her husband's. Jack looked at me. I knew what he was thinking.

And soon I'll come to kill you.

"You said the voice had a slight accent," Jack continued. "You didn't otherwise recognize or place it, did you?"

"No."

Jack sat down next to me. I gave a quick, covert look at my watch. It was eight.

"Would anyone like coffee?" Marian Rusher asked. She made a motion to rise.

"I'd prefer it if you stayed here, Mrs. Rusher," Jack said.

She looked at him for a moment, startled. Then she nodded slowly. "Of course."

Judge Rusher folded his hands over his midsection. He put his head back and looked at the ceiling. His eyes were half-closed. I was sure, however, that he wasn't dozing.

Jack excused himself and left the room, presumably to make another circuit of the house.

The front doorbell rang. Marian Rusher and I jumped slightly. The judge's eyes opened fully. Apart from that, he didn't stir. We heard the front door open and shut. Then voices in the foyer. Then footsteps in the hall.

Five minutes later, Jack returned. I raised my eyebrows at him.

"Reinforcements," he said, with a small grin. He tilted his head toward the foyer. "Paul O'Donnell's going to be out there. Linda's got the back of the house."

"Appreciate it," Judge Rusher said.

"No trouble," Jack replied. He sat down again beside me. There was a small clock on the mantel. Its tick seemed excessively loud in the quiet room. Nobody seemed much inclined to light conversation. Or any kind of conversation.

Marian Rusher picked a magazine off the coffee table, glanced at the cover, and put it back. She folded her hands in her lap.

"Want to improve the shining hour by reading my fan mail?" I said to Jack.

"Yeah, why not?"

I took the bulky manila envelope from beneath my arm and handed it to him. Mrs. Rusher was too well-bred to look openly curious, but I could read the question in her eyes. I explained about the contents of the envelope.

"How awful," she murmured.

There was a tremendous crashing, shattering noise from the rear of the house. Marian Rusher let out a short, startled scream. Jack hurled the envelope aside and sprang to his feet. "Liz," he said. "Get behind this. Mrs. Rusher, Judge, behind that." The Rushers gaped at him. *"Move,"* he yelled. *"Now."*

I yanked the camelback sofa at an angle away from the wall and scrambled into the V-shaped opening between the two. Rusher put his arm around his wife and hustled her and himself behind the love seat. "Elwood," I heard Marian Rusher say in a frightened voice. There was another splintering crash. Jack was out of the room running.

I threw myself flat on the floor.

I heard gunfire, and my heart gave a huge, hard thump. I fumbled with the clasp on my purse. There was another shot. And another. The front door exploded open with a bang.

I got my purse open and slid my hand inside it. My fingers closed around the butt of the gun.

There was a stampede of footsteps in the foyer and hall. Male and female voices. Loud. Screaming. Yelling.

I drew the gun, very slowly, from my purse.

There was a six-inch space between the bottom of the sofa

and the floor. I peered through it. I saw someone run in and out of the front drawing room. Or someone's ankles and shoes.

I could feel the floorboards beneath me vibrating minutely.

The hand that was holding the gun was damp. The barrel felt greasy against my palm.

There was another shuddering crash, as if someone had kicked in a second door somewhere.

I saw more movement in the outer drawing room.

I heard sirens.

Moving in quarter-inch increments, I pushed upright. I held the gun down alongside my leg.

My breathing was ragged and heavy. I made an effort to control it. Perspiration beaded between my breasts and prickled under my arms. Fright sweat.

The yelling in the hall seemed less frenzied.

As I raised my head above the back of the sofa, Jack appeared in the drawing-room archway. His gun was in his hand, and his chest was heaving. We stared at each other. "Liz," he said.

The sirens were quite close now. I let out a long, shuddering sigh.

"Can I come out?" I said.

Jack nodded.

The sirens screeched to a dying halt in front of the house.

"Judge," Jack said, "it's all right now."

There was a thumping noise from behind the love seat. Judge Rusher rose, ponderously. He held a hand down to his wife. I slipped the gun back into my purse and came out from behind the sofa.

Jack wiped at his face with his free hand. Then he put away his own gun.

I went to the archway. The hall was full of cops, in blue and plainclothes. I noticed Gloria among them, and remembered what I'd said to her about a quiet night.

I looked at Jack. He nodded again, answering my unspoken question.

Judge Rusher stood before the fireplace, Marian by his side. He had his arm around her. She seemed to be trembling very slightly. Like all of us. Jack included.

"What happened?" Rusher said.

"He came through the French doors in your kitchen," Jack said.

"*Through?*"

Jack swiped again at his face. "Right through the glass. That was the crash we heard. He must have been coked to the eyeballs."

"Good God."

Jack shook his head slightly. "Nobody makes a move like that unless they're flying, Judge. Maybe the autopsy will tell."

"He's dead?"

"Officer Marshak shot him." Jack took a deep breath. "He came at her with a machete."

What little color remained in Marian Rusher's face fled. "Sweet Jesus," Rusher muttered.

I started past Jack. He put a restraining hand on my shoulder. "It's not a good idea," he said.

I shook my head violently. "No. If it's over, I want to see for myself. If I can write about it, I can look at it."

Jack stared at me for a moment. Then he took his hand from my shoulder.

I went into the hall. Linda Marshak was sitting on the bottom step of the staircase rising to the upper floors. Gloria sat next to her, her arm around Marshak. Marshak's face was wide-eyed and frozen. Her freckles stood out like liver spots.

I walked through a group of cops down the hall to the kitchen. There were more cops there, enough so that at first I didn't see what lay on the floor.

I brushed past two plainclothes people. A blast of cold air cut through the kitchen from the shattered French doors.

He was dressed all in black—jeans, turtleneck sweater, leather jacket, running shoes, and watch cap. He was on his back. His chest was a sodden mess. My head buzzed giddily, and I swallowed hard.

The slack face of the corpse was the face of the man in the Boston P.D. photographs.

A foot or so away from his right hand lay a short-handled instrument with a long shiny blade, squared off at the end.

I turned and walked out of the kitchen.

I sat in the drawing room with the Rushers while the police did what they had to do. I didn't bother to watch when they trundled Cyprian Lord's body in a bag out the front door. I'd seen all I needed.

At ten-thirty, Jack came into the drawing room. "We'll get out of here in a minute," he said. "First I want you to read something."

He held out a sheet of paper by the corner, using a tweezers. He laid it on the coffee table. I leaned forward to look at it.

"What is it?" I asked.

"Something that was found among Lord's possessions." Jack sounded as if he were talking not to me but to the Channel Five news team. "Don't touch it," he added.

I scowled at the unnecessary admonition and bent closer to the tabletop. What was written on the paper appeared to be a list.

It was.

Of names.

Albert Johnson's was at the top. Beneath that was Cassandra Stewart's. Beneath that was Elwood P. Rusher's. Beneath that, Gordon Crane's—Willie Walters's defense lawyer. I didn't recognize the name following that.

Near the bottom of the list was mine. Under that, Jack's. "You win," I said.

"I have to go to the station," Jack said.

"For how long?"

"Oh, honey. I don't know. Could be a couple of hours."

I closed my eyes. "I'm so tired. Do I *have* to come with you?"

"I'd like it better if you did."

"Oh, God, Jack. Cyprian Lord is dead. What's going to happen to me if I go back to your place and stay there by myself for an hour or so? Willie Walters isn't going to send out a replacement assassin after me tonight."

I thought, but didn't say, that I was also sick of being protected.

Jack's face got that closed, tight look. "It would be better if you came with me to the station."

I shook my head.

Jack blew out a long breath. "Okay," he said. "Okay. How about we compromise?"

I looked at him.

"I'll take you back to my place now. But I'll also ask Gloria or Mike or one of the patrol people, whoever can get free quickest, to keep you company."

"Don't they all have better things to do than babysit me?"

"No," Jack said shortly. "They don't."

The Rushers walked us to the front door, almost as if we'd been their dinner guests. The judge shook hands with me. So did Mrs. Rusher.

"You take care of yourself, young lady," Rusher said.

I smiled. "I'll try."

Mrs. Rusher said, "I'll look forward to reading your articles."

"Thank you."

The judge held out his hand to Jack. "I'm grateful to you and your department for what you did tonight."

"Our pleasure," Jack said. He paused, and then added, "Sorry about your kitchen doors."

Marion Rusher laughed. The sound was light and astonishingly free of any trace of hysteria. "Don't mention it."

She had recovered quickly.

Hadn't we all?

We drove back to Jack's house in mostly silence. As we pulled into his driveway, he said, "I talked to Gloria. She should be here in fifteen minutes."

"Okay."

We got out of the car and walked up to the front door. The apartment lights were on, courtesy of the landlord. We went inside. Lucy met us at the door, grinning and wagging. I patted her absently.

"I'll take her out when I get back," Jack said.

"Whatever."

While he walked around the premises, checking that all was secure, I went to the bathroom. I hadn't been for about seven hours and it was a relief. As I was washing my hands, I deliberately avoided my reflection in the mirror over the sink. I knew I must look ghastly.

Jack and I met back in the living room. We gazed at each other for a moment.

"Have we closed the books on this one?" I said.

He smiled wearily. "I hope to hell we have."

He gave me a light kiss on the forehead and left. I locked the front door behind him. I heard his car start up and back out of the driveway.

In addition to turning on the lights and feeding Lucy, Jack's landlord had retrieved the newspapers from the front steps and put them on the coffee table. I'd already read today's *Times*

and *Herald*. The *Globe* I hadn't gotten to yet. Maybe there'd
be a funny Diane White column. I could use a laugh. I grabbed
the paper and let myself fall back onto the couch. Lucy lay
heavily on the floor and grunted softly. Maybe she knew how
I felt.

Diane wasn't in today's paper. The first section was full of
stuff about the Boston School Committee and the Central
Artery and who among the gubernatorial candidates was currently sucking on his foot. The world and national news was
the same crap as in the *Times*.

On the third page of the Metro section was a short piece
that drew my eye like an iron filing to a magnet. The headline
read PROBE INTO NEW HAMPSHIRE CULT CONTINUES. I sat up a
little straighter to read the article.

It was of course about Ray and Ella Mae Bamford and the
Conventicle of Saints. It began with a reference to the fact
that the New Hampshire Attorney General's Office was still
actively pursuing them. Their tax returns for the past five years
had been subpoenaed. Investigators were still posing questions
about the ailing Conventiclers who'd died following Ray Bamford's directive to spend a night alone in the woods.

Ray himself had issued a brief statement to the press that
the New Hampshire Attorney General and his investigators
were minions of Satan, as were the mockers and sinners of
the media. He added further that all these forces of the
Antichrist would surely meet with swift and dreadful punishment.

The kind that Matt Aherne had?

I still couldn't get it out of my head that Matt's auto accident
hadn't been an accident.

The article ended with the note that the Conventicle was
now a computerized operation. This had enabled Ray and Ella
Mae to expand their mailing list geometrically. Ray claimed
that the Conventicle was growing day by day. By which he

probably meant his sucker list of donors was growing day by day.

Jesus, how stupid could people be? I threw the paper on the floor in disgust. Lucy raised her head and gave me a startled look.

"Never mind," I said. "*You're* not a dummy. In fact, you're smarter than most people."

She thumped her tail on the rug in apparent agreement.

I looked at my watch. A quarter of an hour had passed since Jack had left. Gloria should be here momentarily.

Feeling restless, I got up. I glanced at the crumpled newspaper. Perhaps I should give Theresa Aherne a call tomorrow. Just to check on how she was doing. And the kids.

It would be good to know if she'd heard anything at all from the Conventicle since Matt's funeral.

In my mind was a graven image of Ray Bamford sitting outside the church smiling through the windshield of his Mercedes.

I went to the kitchen, Lucy trailing me. I wasn't at all hungry and I wasn't thirsty, but I ought to have something to eat and drink. Tea and toast, maybe. Gloria might like some tea, too.

There were two slices of oatmeal bread left. I crumpled the wrapper and threw it into the trash. I put the bread in the toaster.

I was filling the kettle when I heard a loud bang. I jumped; Lucy's ears shot up and she barked once. I turned off the water and stood listening, my free hand tight on the edge of the counter.

The bang was repeated. Seemed to be coming from nearby and outside. Sounded like wood hitting wood. I frowned. Then I set the kettle on the counter. I leaned over the sink and peered out the window above it.

The window looked out onto a small, screened-in porch. I

pressed my forehead against the glass, waiting for my eyes to adjust to the darkness without. I heard the bang again.

The screen door that led from the porch to the back yard was loose and swinging in the wind. It did that frequently. The landlord had promised to fix it shortly.

There was a stack of folded-up lawn chairs on the porch. I could shove them against the screen door and keep the damn thing shut that way. Otherwise, it would bang to beat the band all night long.

Lucy was curled up under the table with her muzzle on her forepaws. Watching discreetly for the toast to pop, no doubt, in the hope I'd give her a crust.

The cold air hit me like a fist as I opened the kitchen door. I shivered, and scuttled across the porch to the stack of lawn chairs. I heard Lucy bark again.

The very first time I tried to roller-skate I fell backward and hit my head. The only way I can describe the pain is that it sort of crackled.

Like it was doing now. Some kind of crazy yellow light went off inside my skull, and then flashed again before my eyes. Just before I somersaulted into the big black hole, I heard somebody say, "Didn't I tell you I'd always know where to find you? And that soon I'd come to kill you?"

When I regained consciousness, I was lying not on the wooden slats of the porch deck but on a tile floor. I lay motionless, waiting for things to focus. The tiles were cold against the side of my face. The back of my head throbbed. When my vision cleared, I saw the pedestal of a toilet a foot away from me.

I sat up slowly, feeling dizzy and weak. I took a deep breath. Dizziness changed to nausea. I lurched on my knees for the toilet.

When I'd finished, I sat with my back against the tub, my eyes closed. The sick feeling began to pass. I staggered to my feet and over to the sink. After I'd rinsed my mouth, I drank some cold water to get the bile out of my throat.

I looked around me. The bathroom was high-ceilinged, with an old-fashioned frosted glass casement six feet above the tub. The fixtures were all modern. I'd never been in it before. But I knew whose it was.

I opened the door. He was standing on the other side of it, of course, waiting. I looked at him.

"You," I said.

He smiled. Oh, how he smiled.

12

An immense, incapacitating giddiness swept over me again, and I started to crumple. He caught me as I fell. Then he picked me up and carried me down the hall. He was very strong.

The light was on in the room he took me to. It was a bedroom, sparely furnished. An oak bureau against one wall. A queen-sized brass bed. Beside it, a night table. He put me on the bed. Then from his pocket he took a pair of handcuffs. He snapped one of the bracelets around my left wrist, the other to the bedstead railing. He stood over me, looking down at me. His face was neutral, almost bland.

"Why?" I said.

"You know," he said.

I nodded. The movement made my head hurt more.

"I'll be right back," he said. "Oh, by the way. If you're thinking of screaming, the walls and ceilings have been sound-proofed. And this house is set very far back from the street. I need quiet for my work. No one will hear you. Why do you think I brought you here?"

Through a haze, I watched him leave the room. Then I lay back and closed my eyes. I felt about as strong as a worn-out dishcloth. My stomach heaved again. God, I thought, let me please not puke all over myself.

When the sickness receded, I opened my eyes. Tentatively, I moved my left arm. I found I could raise it about eighteen inches, as high as the post I was shackled to would permit.

I looked at the bedside table. No phone on it. If one had been there, he'd probably unplugged and removed it earlier in preparation for . . . tonight's events. There was nothing on the top of the table but a computer manual. His bedtime reading?

I moved my legs sideways with a wriggling motion.

When he returned, I was sitting on the edge of the bed.

"Feeling better?" he said.

"Somewhat."

He sat down next to me. I didn't shrink away from him. I wasn't about to give him that thrill.

"You know, you've been very easy to keep track of these past few weeks," he said.

"Have I?"

"You and your boyfriend are quite the creatures of habit. By the way, the cop did an outstanding job of guarding you." He smiled. "But I knew that if I were patient, sooner or later I'd get you alone."

"Well, you did," I said. "Whoopee for you."

He only smiled some more. "Would you like a drink?"

"No, thanks," I said. "It's bad for someone who's just suffered a head injury to consume liquor."

He laughed. "You think that will matter in a while?" He patted my thigh. "I'll get something for us both. Then we can talk." He rose.

My leg tingled where he'd touched it.

Alone again, I stared at the wall opposite. The window in the center of it was curtained. I wondered what floor of the building we were on. Tied down as I was, I was in no position to be making death-defying leaps from second- or third-story windows.

The look of the bathroom suggested that I was in a rehabbed Victorian house. At the most, those were generally three-floor buildings. People tended to have their bedrooms in the upper stories. If the third floor of this place were attics or dormered rooms, that meant I was on the second floor. About fifteen to twenty feet up. A survivable fall.

Of course, this house could also have been broken up into condos or apartments. In which case, I could be on the first floor.

What did it matter? I wasn't going to go over a windowsill dragging a bed behind me.

With my free hand, I slid open the night-table drawer. Empty but for a book of matches and a box of tissues.

He returned with a glass in either hand. He offered me one, filled with colorless liquid and ice. When I didn't accept it, he set it on the night table. He sipped his own drink. Bourbon or scotch or rye, by the look of it. Or maybe a brandy.

"Talk," he said. "Talk to me."

I looked at him. "What is there to say?"

He smiled. "A great deal. A great deal."

I looked away from him, at the muslin-curtained window in the white wall.

"Tell me about the writing business," he said. "What's it like to be a famous author?"

I turned back to him. Our eyes met. "Nice place you have here," I said.

A little grin played around the corners of his mouth. "You like it? You haven't seen all of it."

"I'm sure the rest is in perfect hi-tech taste."

He inclined his head, mock graciously. "Thank you."

"Do you have the whole house?"

"I *own* the whole house. This floor is my apartment. I have a tenant downstairs."

"How nice for you," I said.

He laughed. We were playing a game he enjoyed.

I nodded at the manual on the night table. "Where's your computer setup?" I asked.

"Down the hall. In the spare bedroom."

"Again, how nice."

"I like it."

"Who's your tenant?"

"Nobody you'd know. Someone in my line of work." He grinned. "He likes quiet too. Even more than I do."

I shivered. I didn't want to. But I couldn't control it.

"Chilly?" he asked.

I nodded. Better he should think I was cold rather than scared. I was both.

"I'll turn up the heat," he said. "I want you to be comfortable."

He got up and went to the thermostat above the light switch on the wall by the door. He flipped it up a few notches. Then he came back to sit alongside me. The mattress sagged a little beneath his weight. He was a big man as well as a strong one.

He sipped his drink, then set the glass on the night table, using the computer manual as a coaster. "I've been looking forward to tonight," he said. His tone was musing. "I planned the whole thing very well. But it took a lot of, um, self-control. My first impulse was just to come after you. But when I thought about it, I realized how much better it would be if I, ah, extended the procedure."

"You mean toyed with me for a while," I said.

He shrugged. "That's one way of putting it. Tell me—what did you think when you got the first letter?"

It was my turn to shrug. "Nothing much. I just figured the sender was some half-mad loser."

He laughed. "Sure you did. You must have gotten worried when the rest of them started arriving, though. I know you did. You moved in with your boyfriend."

"Why not?"

"Why not indeed?"

I thought about making a fist of my free hand and swinging

it up quickly into his face. If I punched hard enough, I could probably break his nose. That would at least temporarily incapacitate him.

But I couldn't hit and run, so to speak, shackled as I was to the bed. And when he'd recovered from whatever injury I'd managed to inflict on him, he'd be in such a blind rage that he'd . . .

No. Forget it.

He leaned back on the bed, propping himself up with his elbows, and surveyed me. "When did you figure out it was me?" he said.

"A while ago," I replied. "It was pretty damn obvious."

"Oh, was it, now?"

"Of course it was. I had some doubts and questions occasionally. Even this afternoon I was wondering about you. But on some level, I was always sure it was you."

"Your cop doesn't think it's me," he said.

"How would you know what he thinks?"

He only smiled.

I looked at my left wrist. "Where'd you get the handcuffs? That place on Mass. Avenue that sells the kinky sex apparatus?"

He laughed. "No, I got them in a place far away from here. In a city where nobody knows me. I told you I planned this whole thing very carefully. Want me to tell you about it?"

I said nothing.

"Where's your writer's curiosity?" he jibed. "I'd have thought you'd want to hear every detail."

"Not particularly," I said.

He put a hand on my right arm. For a moment it rested there lightly. Then it squeezed. "You'll listen if I feel like telling you."

I sat perfectly still, trying not to react visibly to his gesture or his words.

He released my arm. "I was watching you this afternoon,

you know. I saw you leave the police station and go to the newspaper store. I thought of taking you then. In that crowd, it wouldn't have been hard. Also there would have been something very nice about snatching you right out from under the cop's nose."

"Why didn't you, then?"

"Oh, I don't know. Call it prolonging the anticipation."

"Uh-huh."

"You'd be surprised, the number of times I was beside you or behind you or in front of you. And not that far away from you at any time, either."

"Must have been boring, following me around like that."

"No," he said. "Not at all. I would think about what I was going to do to you when I finally got you."

I nodded.

"You know," he continued, "the night I shot at you and the cop, I wasn't trying to hit either one of you."

"I figured that," I said. "It was just part of the game, wasn't it?"

He looked at me for a moment. "You're not dumb, are you?"

"No," I said. "I never was."

"Of course not," he agreed. "You couldn't be stupid and write the way you do. It pains me to admit it, but you do write well. When you're not writing shit." He raised himself slightly from the bed. "People who write shit have to be prepared to take shit. Or worse than shit."

He sat up, reached across me, took his glass from the night table, and drank from it. He looked at my glass. "Your ice is melting."

"I'm not thirsty," I said.

"Suit yourself." He finished his drink and set the glass back down on the night table, next to mine. Then he got up and walked over to the dresser. He pulled open the top drawer and burrowed in its contents. Then he turned back to me.

In his hand was a gun. He raised his arm and pointed it at me. "Sig Sauer," he said. "Nine millimeter."

The hole in the barrel of the pistol looked like a round black eye. "You have a license, I hope," I said. I knew he didn't.

He laughed. "Right. Sure." He lowered his arm. Then he turned the gun around to show me the bottom of the barrel. "It's not loaded now. See? No clip."

He put the gun back in the dresser, placing clothing over it. Then he shut the drawer. He walked over to the night table and picked up his glass.

"When I broke into your apartment, it wasn't just to leave the doll there. I wanted to show you how vulnerable you were. And how easy it would be for me to do . . . whatever I wanted, whenever I wanted."

There was no gloat or menace in his voice. It was calm. Almost reflective.

"I stayed there for a while that night. I walked around. I looked through all your stuff. Your desk, your closets, your dresser. Of course, your dresser." He rolled the glass between the palms of his hands. "I was careful not to disturb anything. I wore gloves."

He sat down next to me, quite close. I could feel the warmth of his body.

"There was justice in that, I thought." He tilted his head and looked at me. "In me invading your privacy. Now you know what it's like, in a way. Only what you did to me was worse."

Because there was nothing to say to that, I said nothing. Side by side, he and I sat in the thick silence of the bedroom. Not quite silence, actually. I could hear, very faintly, traffic sounds. The muted wail of a fire engine. The room we were in must be in the front of the house, facing the street. The keen of the distant siren diminished and died. It was a sound you got used to hearing in Cambridge. The city was mostly old wooden buildings. They were always catching fire. When they burned, they went up like torches.

Something slid into my mind. The seed of an idea.

I held myself very still as it germinated and took root.

"It's time for us to talk seriously," he said.

I glanced quickly, covertly, at the night table. "About what?"

"About what you did to me."

"I didn't do anything to you."

"You wrote about me, you bitch."

I was thinking about how I could get into that night-table drawer. It would have to be when he was out of the room.

Would he leave the room again?

He had finished his drink. Maybe he'd want another. Men his size had a good capacity for liquor. More of it wouldn't impair his faculties. Or his ability to do whatever he was planning. Maybe just enhance the enjoyment of it.

"You're not paying attention. I repeat, you wrote about me, you bitch."

I shrugged. "You were a good subject." My mind was busy elsewhere.

He set his glass carefully on the floor. Then he hit me across the side of the face, backhanded, hard enough to send me flying backward and sideways into the headboard of the bed. The bed moved along with the violent action.

He pressed me down into the mattress, a hand on each of my shoulders. "Don't you fuck with me," he said. "You're in no position to fuck with me."

His face was close enough to mine so that I could feel the damp heat of his breath. And smell on it the odor of scotch. His hands pressed harder, immobilizing my upper body. We stared at each other for a few seconds. Then he let go of my left shoulder and raised himself slightly. He lowered his right hand and, with the index finger, traced a slow "x" on my chest, starting at the end of either collarbone and moving down to the ribs. "You know what I'm going to do to you," he said. "You saw the doll."

I was silent.

He released my other shoulder and sat up. I lay flat, watching him.

"Let me show you something," he said. He reached into his pocket and took from it an object that looked like a six-inch-long black bone cigar. He pressed the side of it with his thumb. Something a little broader than a stiletto shot out of the handle. He held it about four inches away from my eyes.

I didn't breathe.

"You know how strong this is?" he said. "How sharp? It can cut through wood. Just think of what it will do to little chest bones and tendons."

He pressed the button on the hilt of the knife. The blade retracted. He put the knife back in his pocket.

"Let me show you something else," he said. He rose and stood gazing down at me for a moment. Then he left the room.

I wrenched myself upright. My heart was hammering hard enough to shake my whole body. When I could no longer hear his footsteps, I leaned forward and yanked open the night-table drawer. I grabbed the matchbook and slid the drawer shut. Then I shoved the matches into my right hip pocket.

What I was going to do might kill me rather than save me.

I would rather die by my own hand than his.

When he came back to the bedroom, I was sitting hunched over, my arms crossed and pressed to my chest. I didn't look up at him. He stood before me, waiting for me to do so.

Several seconds passed.

He put his hand under my chin and yanked up my head. Something flashed before my eyes.

It was a butcher's knife. The blade was a foot long and two inches wide at its base. It had the unmistakable dull gleam of high-carbon steel.

"Do I have to tell you what this can do?"

I felt as if I were trying to breathe underwater without an oxygen tank. "No," I said.

"Right. Of course not." He sat down beside me. "I'd like to do it while you were conscious and could watch me. And feel it. At least the first part of it. But that would make a mess in here I could never clean up. I can't see myself putting a bloody mattress out on the sidewalk for the garbage collection. So I'll have to knock you out and put you in the bathtub and do it there."

He rose.

"Think about it," he said. "I have some things to do."

I could barely hear his voice over the buzz in my head.

He turned and walked out of the room. He held the knife down by his side.

I squeezed my eyes shut and bent forward to put my head between my knees. I stayed that way until I was sure I wouldn't pass out again. Then I straightened up and sucked in a couple of long, hard breaths. The buzzing subsided and the room came back into focus.

I jammed my hand into my hip pocket and yanked out the matchbook. My fingers were shaking so that I dropped it on the floor. I reached down and snatched it up. Then I sat listening.

There were no footsteps in the hall. Nor could I hear any noises coming from anywhere else in the apartment. He *had* done a good job of soundproofing the place.

What "things" was he doing?

I looked up at the ceiling. In its center was a light fixture. Nothing else. No smoke detector. Good. Probably there was one in the hall. By law, there had to be.

The distance between the bed and the window was about five feet. I pushed the night table further down the wall. Then I stuck the matchbook in my shirt pocket and got up, very slowly. The handcuff chain gave me virtually no leeway. I stood in the empty space where the night table had been. I leaned sideways, reaching out with my right arm toward the window.

No matter how hard I strained, my fingers fell short of the hem of the curtain by a good foot.

Tears of frustration and desperation prickled behind my eyes. I made a futile pawing motion at the window.

Okay. Get a grip on yourself.

I straightened and took another deep, shaking breath. Then I turned, grabbed the headboard of the bed with both hands, and pulled.

The bed dragged away from the wall with a screech of casters on the wide-planked pine floor. I yanked at it again, staggering backward, hauling it along with me.

I was able to move the bed about two feet before one of the casters caught in a knothole.

Two feet was more than enough. Just to make sure, I reached out and grabbed for the curtain. I crumpled a fistful of muslin. It felt like God's raiment. If I could have kissed it, I would have.

I didn't. I released the curtain and fished the matchbook from my shirt pocket. I turned back to the bed and transferred the matchbook to my left hand. I flicked it open with my thumb. I ripped out a match with my right hand and struck it. It sparked and I pointed it downward for the flame to catch on to the stem. When it had, I swiveled around and leaned toward the window.

I probably moved too fast and created a draft. Whatever, the match flame shrank and expired. I let the dead match drop, cursing myself. I turned back to the bed to repeat the process.

Match number two exploded like a tiny Roman candle and fizzled out against the flint.

Match number three caught. I let it burn halfway down the stick before I turned back to the window.

This is insane, what you're doing.

Oh, yeah? What's the alternative?

I held the match to the bottom of the curtain. The material caught just as the match itself burned down into my fingertips. I didn't even feel the sting.

A tiny little flame licked at the muslin. It flared and then subsided into a smolder.

I lit three matches simultaneously, stretched out, and with them ignited the outer edge of the second curtain panel. Then I turned to the bed and ripped back its cover. I grabbed the pillow nearest me and set fire to its case. When it was going I flung it into the farthest corner of the room.

The bed I pushed and shoved as much back away from the window as I could.

I jerked open the night-table drawer, pulled out the box of tissues, and lit it. That I tossed on top of the dresser.

A grayish puff of smoke billowed out from the window. The flames had eaten three-quarters of the way up the curtain and were dancing around the molding of the window.

I threw back my head and screamed loudly enough to bring my lungs up into my throat. A burst of flame from the curtain shot up the wall to the ceiling. A loud mechanical screech pierced the smoky air. I pulled my shirt up to cover my nose and mouth.

I was shaking so hard I could barely stand. I grabbed hold of the bedpost with my right hand.

Whether it was my scream or the noise of the smoke detector or both that brought him, I don't know. For the barest moment he stood frozen in the bedroom doorway. Then he yelled, "Jesus *Christ.*" He lunged into the room, bent down, and swept a small area rug from the floor. He swung it at the window, beating at the flames.

A thin line of fire ran along the back of the oak dresser. No longer able to breathe, I doubled over.

He was at my side. I felt him grab at my left wrist. The cuff around it dug into my flesh for a moment. Then the bracelet loosened and dropped. He pulled me away from the bed, twisted my left arm behind me, and pushed me in the direction of the door.

The hall was almost as smoky as the bedroom. The smoke detector shrilled unceasingly. We lurched and stumbled past the bathroom into the foyer.

Someone was pounding on the front door. And yelling something incoherent.

Smoke was drifting into the foyer. I drew as much breath as I could and screamed again.

"*Shut up.*" He spun me around and hit me across the side of the face, hard enough so that I staggered back against the foyer wall.

The pounding on the front door became crashing.

He reached into his pocket and took out the knife. He pressed the button on the side and the blade sprang from the hilt. He held it up to my face.

"This way," he said. He dragged me away from the wall and locked his free arm around my neck. He pushed me across the foyer and into the living room. Smoke hung in the air in layers. I bumped into a coffee table and would have sprawled across its top if he hadn't been holding me so rigidly pressed to his own body. We edged around the table and continued our awkward progress across the room, till we came to a door in the rear wall.

"Open it," he said.

Coughing, my eyes tearing, I fumbled for the knob. I could barely see. I hauled back the door. A blast of cold, clean air hit us. He shoved me over the threshold and the two of us stumbled onto a small wooden deck.

Through the bare branches of the trees beyond the deck, the lights of Memorial Drive and the bridge across the Charles sparked and glimmered. Beyond those, the lights of Storrow Drive and the Back Bay townhouses and apartment buildings.

The knife blade was still inches away from my face.

I could hear sirens, quite loud and growing louder. Someone had called the fire department. Probably whoever had been pounding on the front door.

I made a slight noise, like a moan. Then I went limp. I let my head roll back against his shoulder. My lower body sagged forward. I moaned again.

"*Shit*," he muttered. The arm around me loosened as my full weight tugged on it. "*Shit*. Stay conscious, goddamn you." He tried to heave me upright and I let my knees cave completely. As I settled toward the deck floor his hold on me went just marginally more slack.

The sirens were in front of the house now.

I jumped up straight, kicked back with my right foot, and stamped the heel down on the toes of his right foot. Then I whirled around, raised my right hand, and slammed the edge of it down across the bridge of his nose. I made a fist of my left hand and drove it with all my body behind me into his stomach.

I'd thought that would make him drop the knife.

It didn't. He fell back against the door jamb, gasping. Blood ran from his nose.

The fingers of his right hand seemed to tighten around the knife hilt. He raised it.

I was off and running across the deck to the stairs. He heaved himself off the door jamb and after me.

At the bottom of the stairs was a small platform, like a minideck. It was gated. The gate was closed. I kicked at it. It held. I kicked at it again. Then I saw the padlock holding it closed.

I put my hands on the top bar and flung one leg over it.

He grabbed the other leg by the calf. I wrenched it free and hurled myself over the top of the gate.

I landed on my side, rolled once, and staggered to my feet.

Flames ten feet high were shooting up the side of the house.

He came over the gate and landed with a thud behind me.

In front of me was a six-foot-high stockade fence. No way could I vault that. There was more of the same fencing to my left. To the right, the lawn descended in a series of terraces.

I ran to the right.

He was behind me. I could almost hear his breathing.

At the bottom of the last terrace was a thicket of denuded forsythia bushes. I crashed through it. The branches ripped at my face.

Behind the bushes was more stockade fencing. I slammed right up against it. *"Shit!"* I screamed. I hunched over and ran along the narrow corridor between the forsythia and the fence.

I couldn't hear him behind me.

God, he was probably waiting for me at the end of the row of bushes. I turned around and doubled back up the path.

I came to the intersection of the back and side fences and plunged through the hedge onto the lawn.

The whole back yard was lit up as bright as midday by the flames.

I couldn't see him anywhere.

With a huge roaring *whoosh* and a July Fourth explosion of sparks, part of the roof of the house collapsed. The entire upper right side of the house was one solid sheet of fire.

I ran diagonally back up the terraces to the left. There had to be an opening in this goddamn fence *somewhere*.

Where was he?

Oily black smoke roiled up from the house and out across the lawn. The stink of burning pitch and plastic was heavy in the air.

There was a gate in the middle of the fencing on the top left side of the lawn. I hurled myself at it.

It was bolted on the inside. I rammed the bolt back and hit the gate with the palms of both hands. It swung outward onto a driveway. I ran through the opening.

No one was behind me. No one leaped out of the shadows at me.

I ran down the driveway.

There were five fire engines in the street. Three huge streams of water arced upward at the house from different angles. Blue and red flashing lights competed with the orange brilliance of the flames like the strobes in some apocalyptic disco. The sidewalk and the front yard were a Laocoön tangle of hoses.

Where was he?

Two firemen came out of the front door of the house.

"I think somebody's gone back in there!" I screamed at them.

A fireman with an axe was chopping out a second-story window. "Check the house," I screamed up at him. He probably didn't hear me.

I ran toward the nearest truck. Somebody grabbed at my arm. It was a heavyset man of medium height in a slicker and helmet.

"Lady, what—"

"Someone's still in the house!" I shrieked into his face.

He stared at me for a quarter of a second and then released my arm. He turned toward another group of firemen and yelled something at them.

I dodged around the end of the engine, past an ambulance, and into a mob of sightseers. I pushed blindly through the morass of bodies and acrid smoke.

At either end of the block was parked, diagonally, a police cruiser to cut off the flow of any other than emergency vehicle traffic. I ran toward the nearest one.

Beside the front fender of the cruiser stood Sam Flaherty.

"Jesus Christ Almighty," he said.

They found him on the deck off the second floor of the house. He'd only gotten that far before the smoke had overcome him.

He was alive when they brought him down and put him in an ambulance.

The last sparks of the fire were extinguished at 3:08 that morning.

13

Garrett was still alive the next day. They had him in intensive care at Mount Auburn Hospital for about eight hours. Then they moved him to a regular room.

He would, they thought, fully recover shortly.

There was a police guard outside his door.

When he did recover, he would be sent to the state hospital at Bridgewater for twenty days' psychiatric observation.

I got taken to the hospital, too. Not in an ambulance, in a cruiser. In the emergency ward they made me breathe pure oxygen. They also cleaned up the cuts and scratches I'd gotten on my face diving into the forsythia. I had some bruises from being hit that they couldn't do much to treat. They were concerned about me having a concussion from being slugged over the head. They wanted me to stay overnight. I refused. We debated. I won. They told me to take it easy for a week and report back to them immediately if I suffered dizzy spells or double vision or faintness. I said I would.

They released me to Jack.

Three days was all I could take of taking it easy.

On day four I had an after-work drink with Denise Amaral. Except it wasn't really a drink since she wasn't drinking because of her pregnancy and I wasn't drinking because of my possible concussion. Pain in the ass. I would have sold my soul for a vodka martini. You can never have one when it'd taste the best. Like when you've been shot at with no result.

We were on diet Coke.

"Let me get this straight," Denise said. "You torched the *house?*"

I widened my eyes at her. "The bedroom window curtain caught fire because it was too close to the heating unit."

"Uh-huh," she said, returning my stare. "Right. I'll say no more."

"If you don't believe me, ask the fire department. They'll verify it for you."

"I said I'd say no more."

I nodded.

We were in what called itself the sports bar of the Royal Sonesta. Our table was next to the window, affording us a spectacular view of the Charles and Boston. The bar was nearly empty. All the sports fans were apparently disporting themselves elsewhere this evening.

"Why did he go back into the house?" Denise asked.

I spun my glass around on the tabletop. Then I said, "You want my guess?"

"Would I have asked if I didn't?"

"I think he went back in to try and save the work he had in his computer room."

She looked at me for a moment. "You're probably right."

"The work always meant more to him than anything else," I said. I wanted to add, "Which I can understand, because mine does to me, too." But I didn't. To say such a thing wouldn't have been quite truthful. My work *did* mean everything to me. But Jack meant more, for other reasons. There were an infinite number of words in my head that I could put down on paper in whatever order I chose whenever I chose.

The words could be replaced. Jack couldn't.

"You know how Garrett felt about what he did?" I said.

"Yeah." Denise sipped her drink. "I do. I worked with him long enough."

We finished our Cokes. I gestured at the waitress to bring us another round.

"So," Denise said. "So. The whole time you thought it was only one person out to get you, it was really two."

I laughed shortly. "Yeah. A crazy homicidal Jamaican gangster and a crazy homicidal biochemist. And both for similar reasons—the terrible things I said about them in print."

Denise shook her head. "You know, I've always had this mental image of writing for a living being such a civilized, peaceful, quiet kind of career."

"Guess again," I said. "You may have me confused with Emily Dickinson or Edith Wharton."

"Not hardly," she said.

The waitress served us our drinks.

"Ever think of changing careers?" Denise asked.

"You're the second person who's asked me that recently. No."

"No?"

"No." I paused a moment, trying to figure out the exact wording for what I wanted to express. "Denise, what I do now is what I've always wanted to do, all my life. I love it. If I couldn't write, I'd . . . wither or something. There wouldn't be any point in getting out of bed in the morning if there weren't something there waiting for me to write about it."

"Okay."

"If people get mad at me for doing what I do, then so be it. Tough shit."

Denise nodded, and drank some of her Coke.

I patted my handbag. "In any case, I got my gun right here in case any other bozo ever decides to come after me."

She laughed.

The waitress put a bowl of pretzel nuggets in the middle of the table.

Denise said, "Did you ever figure out how Garrett found out about the story you wrote about him?"

I shrugged. "No. All I know is that he *did* read it. There was a copy of it in his computer room. The cops found it when they went in to look around."

She frowned at me. "*That* survived the fire?"

"It was really only the upper right side of the house that was destroyed. The other part—it had a lot of smoke damage. But it was basically intact. His workroom was in the intact part of the house."

"I see."

I put my chin in my hand and looked out at Memorial Drive. The copy of my short story about him wasn't the only artifact related to me that the cops had found in Garrett's workroom. They'd found there a copy of the *Cambridge Monthly* that had printed my article about Dr. Murray Evans.

The photograph of me that had appeared with the piece had been neatly clipped from the page.

The cops had also found a pad of cheap white generic stationery and a bottle of red nail enamel. The shade of the polish was identical to the one that had been used to paint the red cross on the doll Garrett had left in my apartment.

All of the stuff was in the state police now, being analyzed. It would be evidence at the trial. If there would ever be a trial.

Today was Garrett's first day in Bridgewater. God only knew what the shrinks would find inside his head.

"Liz?"

I turned my head away from the window and back to Denise. "What?"

"Can I ask you something else?"

"Sure."

She looked at me very steadily through the dim cocktail-hour light. "If Garrett was going to kill you, why did he bother to rescue you from the fire?"

I was silent for a moment. Then I said, "Probably because he would have found it difficult to explain to the police and the state fire marshal why there was a charred corpse handcuffed to the ruins of a bed. Anyway, if I'd died in the fire, he'd have been deprived of the pleasure of doing me in himself."

"You really think he would have killed you?"

"Oh, yes. I think he hated me more than anyone else on earth. Because I knew what he was inside."

"And you told the world."

"Or at least that part of it that reads short pieces in magazines."

"He was terribly sick," Denise said.

"Yeah. But I think you and Dana Hogan and I were the only people who really knew that. Or could bring ourselves to believe it."

"A lot of other people do, now."

I nodded and drank the rest of my soda.

Denise said, "So why did you bother to save *him* from the fire, then?"

I looked at her. *"I'm* not a murderer."

Four men in suits came into the bar and took a table next to ours. They glanced at us in that casual yet proprietary way that, when I'm in a bad mood, always sets my teeth on edge. When I'm in a good mood, it just makes me snicker.

"Was that the only reason?" Denise asked.

The business guys were laughing about something.

"No," I said.

The cocktail waitress shot over to the businessmen's table to take their drink orders. I couldn't blame her for offering them lightning service. They'd josh with her and leave her a huge tip. She had fabulous legs beneath her black mini.

"What?" Denise said. "What was the other reason?"

I looked again at the window. What I was going to say would

come easier if I could pretend to be speaking to a blank sheet of plateglass rather than to an intelligent and intently alert human being.

"He was somebody I loved once," I said.

There was another burst of laughter from the table next to ours.

Jack picked me up at the Sonesta's main entrance. We made a stop at Aram's Number Two on Cambridge Street to buy a couple of sub sandwiches to take back to his place for dinner. And then we detoured to a liquor store to buy some beer for him.

I held the bag of food on my lap. I looked over at Jack.

"Can we stop at my place?" I asked. "So I can check my phone messages and mail?"

"Sure."

We turned off Cambridge Street onto Prospect.

"You spoke today to the people Garrett worked for at Kendall Associates," I said. "What did you find out from them?"

"That they thought he had problems."

"Oh?" I glanced over at Jack. "Problems of what sort?"

"Sounded like the same ones he had while he was at Bioline. Only more exaggerated, you know? Paranoia about his ideas being stolen."

"Hostility toward women coworkers?"

"Uh-huh."

We turned right onto Hampshire Street.

"Were they going to let him go?" I asked.

"Oh, hell, no. He was very valuable to them. They let him do what he wanted. Make his own hours."

"No wonder he had the time to follow me around."

We stopped for a red light.

"Yeah." Jack said. "No wonder."

His tone was very flat. I knew what was bothering him. The

same thing that had been bothering him since the arrival of the sixth letter. The one that went: *You can try to protect the bitch. But someday, when you're not looking, I'll get her.*

I couldn't repeat over and over again that it wasn't his fault that Garrett had snatched me. I didn't really know what to do.

We drove the rest of the way in silence.

There was an empty parking place two doors down from my house.

The street was dark and empty, as it usually was after dark. A lot of older people lived in this neighborhood, and they didn't go out much in the evening.

I took Jack's arm as we walked up the path to the front door of my building. Just before the steps I stopped, raised my face, and gave him a kiss on the cheek. He smiled at me.

I unlocked the door and we went into the foyer. A huge pile of mail was waiting for me on a small table, put there by the landlord. I scooped it up and we went up to my apartment.

The automatic timer had put on the lights and inside everything was bright and orderly.

"Want me to do a little search and seizure?" Jack asked. "Just to be on the safe side?"

I laughed. "Be my guest."

As he went through the apartment, I listened to my phone messages. Half social. Half business. My friends I'd get back to tonight. The business could wait.

Jack returned to the living room. "All quiet on the western front," he said.

I nodded. "Thank you, love. Don't know what I'd do without you."

"Liz?"

"Yes?"

He looked at me for a few seconds. Then he tilted his head at the couch. "Let's sit down for a moment, okay?"

"Certainly."

We got settled on the couch. I peered at him a bit anxiously.

He shook his head and laughed a little. "You're doing it again."

"Doing what?"

"Giving me that look."

"What look?"

"Like you're waiting for me to fall apart or something."

"Oh, no, Jack—"

He held up his right hand. "Wait; let me go on."

I closed my mouth.

"I'm fine."

"Well, I know *that*—"

"Will you let me finish? Please?"

I nodded.

He took a deep breath. "All right," he said. "I admit, I feel like kind of a horse's ass. But that's my problem. And I'll get over it. Really. So you don't have to treat me like I'm made of glass. Okay?"

I nodded again.

"And I get the feeling you're standing in front of me with a bellows trying to reinflate my ego. You don't have to do that. All right?"

I nodded a third time.

"Let's just go back to being the way we always are."

"There's nothing I'd rather do," I said.

"Good," he said. "That's settled." He leaned forward and kissed me hard on the lips.

"You are one tough bastard," I said.

"Fucking A," he replied. "Keep it in mind."

"I wouldn't dream of forgetting it."

"Okay. Now let's go back to my place and feed the dog and eat our sandwiches."

"Sure." I gestured at the stack of mail on the coffee table. "Mind if I sort through that crap there first?"

"Go ahead." He leaned back on the couch.

I picked up the bundle of mail and dropped it in my lap.

Jack said, "I got the report on Matt Aherne's accident today from the New Hampshire State Police."

I looked up sharply. "Oh? And?"

"It was just that, an accident. No sign at all that the car had been tampered with."

"None at all?"

"No."

"I see." I sighed raggedly.

"What's wrong?"

"Oh, I'd just love to see Ray Bamford really nailed, that's all."

"Well, the New Hampshire A.G.'s office is still after him."

"And let's devoutly hope they get him." I paused. "Jack?"

"Yes?"

"I want to do something for Matt's kids."

"What's that?"

"I'm going to take five hundred dollars from my savings account and buy them some bonds."

He frowned thoughtfully. "That's a good idea. I'll throw in another five hundred."

I stared at him. "But . . . you didn't know Matt. I mean, that's wonderful of you, honey, so generous, but . . . why?"

"Why not?"

I smiled. "Why not, indeed? Okay. Thank you."

"My pleasure."

"Well—" I gestured at the mail in my lap. "Let me hurry and riffle through this junk so we can be on our way."

The mail was thrilling. Some magazines, which I handed to Jack. A VISA bill. A gas bill. An electric bill. Something with URGENT stamped all over it that turned out to be a frenzied plea from a time-share outfit enjoining me to come and collect the fabulous prize they were reserving for ME JUST ME. A letter from my mother. An invitation to a gallery opening. Another letter, postmarked yesterday.

I ripped open the envelope. Inside was a sheet of fine-quality bond, almost as heavy as parchment, folded in thirds. Unusual weight and texture. I rubbed the paper between my fingers.

The text of the document was handwritten in flowing, spiked script. It had no date. It bore no salutation. It had neither closure nor signature. The writing was unfamiliar.

It began, "You bitch . . ."

ABOUT THE AUTHOR

SUSAN KELLY's first Liz Connors novel, *The Gemini Man*, was nominated by the World Mystery Convention for an Anthony Award for best first novel of 1985, and was one of the top ten books in the National Mystery Readers poll for the same year. She has a doctorate in medieval literature from the University of Edinburgh and has been a consultant to the Massachusetts Criminal Justice Training Council as well as a teacher of crime-report writing at the Cambridge, Massachusetts, Police Academy. She lives in Cambridge, and is at work on her next Liz Connors novel.